Within These

Haunted

Walls

A Horror Novel By

Kit Lewis

WITHIN THESE HAUNTED WALLS

CONTENTS

PROLOGUE

As the early 1950s dwindled in the dark recesses of the Appalachian Mountains, a rustic cabin stood secluded among the dense, whispering pines. Here, a family eked out a living, closely tied to the ancient spirit of the land.

On a crisp evening under a bright full moon, Ruby, the matriarch, stepped onto the creaky porch with offerings of food and water. These she placed with care at the steps—a time-honored ritual to honor the spirits believed to roam the deep woods.

Behind her, the door squeaked open, and her daughter Sandra, a sprightly young girl with curious eyes, tiptoed out. "Mama, why we always leavin' food out here?" she asked in a hushed whisper, her voice carrying the twang of their mountain heritage.

"We're showin' respect, darlin'," Ruby explained, her eyes scanning the encroaching dusk. "These mountains hold more'n just critters; they're filled with spirits, old as the hills. We leave these offerings to keep peace, to show we're mindful of 'em."

Absorbing every word, Sandra peered into the shadows that clung to their home. "And the whistlin', Mama? Why can't we whistle after dark?"

Ruby sighed; the weight of the lore heavy in her voice. "That's a darker matter, love. Long ago, there was a man, folks called him Father who lived up top of the mountain in a big ol' house, above a hidden mineshaft. Died, but never rested. Now, he whispers through the trees, trying to lure folks with whistlin'. He gets the young'uns he's taken to do it too—whistlin' to trap more souls. If ever you hear your name on the wind after dark or that whistlin', you never answer. It's him, tryin' to take you away."

The legend of Father, a shadowlike figure once a man, had woven itself deeply into the fabric of local superstition. His presence was marked by eerie whispers and ghostly whistles that floated through the night, seeking to ensnare the unwary. Those who responded were never seen again, believed to be lost forever to his shadowy domain, coerced into perpetuating his sinister whims.

As the night air grew colder, Ruby ushered Sandra back inside, securing the door against the encroaching darkness. The cabin, lit by the soft glow of oil lamps, offered a semblance of safety against the night's chilling tales.

Outside, under the moonlight, the offerings lay untouched, a fragile truce between the living and the spirits of the Appalachian wilderness, while the wind carried a soft, chilling whistle that danced just beyond the edge of sight.

In the late 1800's, nestled in the heart of the Appalachian wilderness, the quaint town of Micaville drew its warmth from the generous spirit of Harold, a cherished elder whose grand estate was a beacon of hospitality. Known for hosting grand parties that filled the air with laughter and light, Harold was more than just a resident—he was a pillar of the community. Without children of his own, he saw the townspeople as his extended family and cherished the nickname "Father" that many had affectionately bestowed upon him. Harold embraced this role with joy, genuinely loving the feeling of being a paternal figure to everyone in Micaville.

Harold's doors—and heart—were always open. Whether hosting festive gatherings or quietly aiding those in need, he personified the spirit of generosity. Whenever misfortune befell a neighbor, Harold was there with a warm smile, ready to offer food, money, or a comforting meal. His sprawling, magnificent home stood not just as his residence but as a symbol of unwavering support and kindness within the community.

However, tragedy struck one fateful year when a devastating fire ravaged Micaville, leaving desolation in its wake. Miraculously, Harold's estate remained untouched by the flames, but the disaster cast a long shadow over his spirit. Despite this darkness, Harold's resolve to support and rebuild the community only grew stronger, proving that even in the face of despair, the bonds of family—blood or not—can illuminate the path to recovery.

Suspicion swirled like the smoke that lingered after the blaze. Whispers spread among the townsfolk that Harold had set the fire, an act of madness or malice that spared only his own lavish home. As the community struggled to rebuild, children began to vanish, one by one, deepening the mystery and fear. Each disappearance was shrouded in whispers, and eyes turned toward Harold, the man who had survived the fire unscathed.

Harold protested his innocence, his voice desperate over the murmur of suspicion. But the town's grief was too great, their need for justice too raw. When the sheriff's child disappeared, it was the final straw. The town's sorrow curdled into rage, and one eerie night, they dragged Harold from the sanctuary of his home. They brought him to the center of what had once been their vibrant town square, now just a charred echo of itself.

Under the ghostly light of the moon, they tied him to a large pole, the wood smelling faintly of smoke. As the flames licked the night sky, the townsfolk began to whistle an old Irish tune, "Marble Halls," a melody that twisted the night with its chilling cheer. Harold's screams pierced the night, mingling with the haunting whistle, and with his last breath, he cursed the town and vowed vengeance upon those who had wronged him.

From that night on, the spirit of Harold, now twisted by the flames of betrayal and the echoes of that eerie tune, haunted the woods. His whispers carried on the wind, calling to the unwary, fueled by a vengeful fury that turned the once benevolent man into a spectral terror, known only as Father. His once grand parties were replaced by gatherings of shadows and mist, his generosity twisted into a malevolent desire to pull the living into his eternal, vengeful game.

A New Beginning

In the autumn of 2024, as leaves turned golden and the air grew crisp, John Harper found himself settled at the kitchen table of their cozy city condo. It was a cool fall afternoon, one that invited reflection with its quiet calm. Spread before him was a stack of third-grade assignments, each page awaiting his red pen's judgment. As he graded, his brow furrowed in concentration, the pen tapping rhythmically against the wooden surface. Meanwhile, the low hum of the evening news played in the background, its stories a stark reminder of the bustling world beyond their tranquil home.

Mary Harper, his wife, bustled around the kitchen, preparing dinner. The tension in the room was intense, a constant undercurrent in their lives lately. Money was tight—too tight. John's job as an elementary school teacher was fulfilling but woefully underpaid, and Mary's part-time work at a local boutique barely covered their mounting expenses.

"How are we supposed to make ends meet with what we make?" Mary asked, her voice edged with frustration as she chopped vegetables. "The bills keep piling up, and we're barely scraping by."

John sighed, setting his pen down and rubbing his temples. "Dammit, I know, Mary. I know. But what can we do? I'm trying my best here."

Mary turned to face him, her expression a mix of anger and desperation. "We need to find a solution. We can't keep living like this. The kids need stability, and we can't even provide that."

Their daughter, Emma, appeared in the doorway, her headphones draped around her neck. She had heard their arguments before, and the familiarity of their raised voices was a bitter comfort. "Are you guys fighting again?" she asked, her tone weary.

"We're just talking, sweetheart," John said, forcing a smile. "Go finish your homework."

Emma rolled her eyes and retreated to her room, muttering under her breath. Her younger brother, Ben, was playing quietly in the living room, the only one seemingly untouched by the growing strain in the household.

As Mary turned back to the stove, John broached a subject they had discussed before but never seriously considered. "What if we sold our place and moved? Got out of the city? There are places where the cost of living is lower, where we could afford a decent life."

Mary shook her head, her knife pausing mid-chop. "You know how I feel about that. I've lived in the city most of my life. I can't imagine moving to the middle of nowhere. And what about the kids? Emma's in high school, for God's sake. It's not fair to uproot her now."

"I know it's a big change," John said, his voice softening. "But maybe it's what we need. A fresh start. A place where we don't have to worry about every little expense, where we can breathe a little easier. We're outgrowing this place anyway. I've been looking at housing prices and we can sell this place for almost a million bucks."

Mary was silent for a moment, considering his words. She was a country bumpkin at heart, born in Northern California, and lived her younger years in a small town just a few hours north. But she left to live in the city when she was around twelve years old, and she found comfort in the bustling streets of San Francisco. With inflation and the high prices of living, the relentless stress of their financial situation was wearing her down. She glanced at John, seeing the weariness in his eyes, the toll that their constant struggle was taking on him. "I just... I don't know, babe. It's such a huge step."

"I get it, honey. But think about it. We could find a place where the kids can run around, where we can have a little garden, where we can live instead of just survive."

Days turned into weeks as summer break rolled around, and the conversation continued to weigh on Mary's mind. The arguments about money persisted, each one chipping away at her resolve. Finally, after yet another fight over unpaid bills and mounting debts, Mary sighed and looked at John. "Okay," she said quietly. "Let's do it. Let's look for a place out of the city."

John was relieved, and for the first time in months, there was a glimmer of hope in his eyes. "You won't regret this, honey. I promise."

The search began, and it wasn't long before they found it— an old Victorian farmhouse in the small town of Micaville, nestled in the Appalachian Mountains. It was a far cry from their cramped little condo, with enough space for the kids to play and a cost of living that seemed almost too good to be true. The realtor told them the house had been vacant for years, its history a patchwork of interesting tales and rich history. But John was undeterred, eager for the fresh start it promised.

Mary had always felt a certain apprehension towards old houses and the secrets they seemed to harbor. Growing up, she spent her summers at her aunt and uncle's place on Mountain House Road in the quaint town of Hopland. The house was a grand old Victorian, its stature imposing and filled with stories that seemed to seep from its very walls.

Those summers were marked by a series of eerie events that left her uneasy: doors would slam shut without any discernible cause, mysterious phone calls would pierce the silence of the night, answered only by unsettling heavy breathing on the other end, and shadows flickered at the periphery of her vision as if something—or someone—was always lurking just out of sight. The family dog once, in an inexplicable frenzy, leaped from the second-story balcony into the bed of a pickup truck below, as though desperate to escape an invisible pursuer.

The bathroom mirror seemed to reveal more than her reflection; often, she would glimpse what appeared to be ghostly figures shifting in the shadows behind her. The sight was so disturbing that she began to dread her nighttime visits to the bathroom, sometimes to the point of avoiding them altogether, often with embarrassing results. These experiences ingrained in her a deep wariness of the storied pasts that old homes carry with them.

This house wasn't just any old building; it stood on land steeped in history, a site where Pomo Indians once hunted and fished, and which later passed into the hands of Spanish settlers. It had seen the comings and goings of stagecoaches and later, the North Pacific Railroad. Even President William McKinley had once been a guest, sleeping in a grand bed that still stood in one of the upstairs bedrooms, a relic from his tour of the region in the late

1890s. Originally built in the late 1880s as a stagecoach stop, the storied and now uninhabitable Grand Victorian mansion was a local landmark.

Despite its rich history, the mansion had an intense sense of the uncanny. Almost everyone who stayed there experienced something inexplicable, something eerie that lingered in the air like a whisper from the past. Those haunting summers had left an indelible mark on Mary. Even years later, as an adult, the experiences solidified her belief in the paranormal, a belief rooted in the very walls of that old mansion where history and mystery walked hand in hand.

"This place better not give me a creepy feeling, or we're turning around and coming right back to California," Mary said, with an angry look on her face.

"Don't worry honey, we'll be just fine. I don't know why you still believe in all that garbage anyway."

"I've seen them before, I don't know how you cannot believe in the spirit world."

"Jesus, honey, the spirit world? Really? I'm sure you just had a big imagination when you were little, and not so loud, you're going to scare the kids."

"I'm not arguing about this right now."

Ben overheard his parents talking and thought it would be a good idea to hide behind the couch and wait for the perfect opportunity to scare his poor mother. Just as she sat down to relax and calm herself down, Ben leaped up and grabbed onto his mom's shoulders.

"Boo!"

"Shit! Ben, you can't do that. You scared the crap out of me."

Ben rolled over the back of the couch and onto the cushions, jumped up, and ran off chanting, "Mom believes in ghosts, mom believes in ghosts."

Emma overheard the commotion and came back out of her room. She took one glance at her mom's angry face and then over at her brother who was still chanting about mom believing in ghosts.

"Ben, knock it off. You're so immature. Leave mom alone." Emma said, shaking her head and walking back into her room.

Emma was a typical teenager who thought she was just way too cool to be in this household full of old folks and a bratty baby brother, but she also had a big heart.

A New Home

As they packed up their lives and prepared for the move, the family dynamic shifted. There was a sense of anticipation, a cautious optimism that maybe, just maybe, this was the answer to their prayers. Emma was less thrilled, grumbling about leaving her friends behind, while Ben was excited about the adventure ahead.

On the day they left the city behind, the car was packed to the brim with their belongings, and the rest was packed into the moving truck that would meet them there later. John glanced in the rearview mirror at the condo they had called home for so long, then looked over at Mary, who gave him a small, hopeful smile.

"Here we go," John said, starting the engine and pulling out onto the road.

The drive to Micaville was long and winding, taking them deeper into the heart of the mountains. The landscape changed from urban sprawl to dense forests and rolling hills, the air growing crisper with each mile. When they finally arrived, the house stood at the end of a narrow dirt road, its weathered facade and ivy-clad walls a stark contrast to the concrete jungle they had left behind.

As they stepped out of the car and took in their new surroundings, John felt a sense of peace wash over him. "We're home," he said softly, taking Mary's hand in his.

Mary looked at the house, then at her children. "Yes," she said, a note of determination in her voice. "We are."

But as the sun dipped below the horizon, the Harpers would soon learn that every new beginning comes with its own set of challenges—and that some legends are not just stories.

As the Harper family unloaded from their car, Emma's eyes scanned the dilapidated house in front of them. She wrinkled her nose in disdain. "This place is old and dirty. I hate it," she declared, crossing her arms over her chest. "I want to go back to my friends."

Ben, ever the little brother, smirked and nudged her. "You didn't have any friends anyway, Emma."

"Shut up, Ben!" Emma snapped, shoving him back.

"Hey, knock it off, you two," John interjected, stepping between his children. "We're here now, and we're going to make the best of it. Go on, explore the house. There's plenty of room for both of you."

Emma shot a glare at Ben before stomping up the creaky steps and pushing the front door open. Ben followed; his excitement undimmed by his sister's sour mood.

Mary stood by the car, her eyes scanning the property with a mixture of trepidation and disappointment. "Babe, this place... it looks nothing like the pictures. It's going to need a lot of work. And the nearest hospital is almost twenty miles away. What if something happens?"

John put a reassuring arm around her shoulders. "I know it's not perfect, honey. But we can fix it up. I can handle most of the repairs myself, and think about the space. Ten acres! The kids will have so much room to play. It'll be an adventure."

Mary sighed; her eyes still fixed on the house. "I just hope you're right. This is a big change."

"Just try and relax. With the money we got from selling our little condo, we were able to buy this place outright and have enough money left for renovations and we won't have to worry about bills for a very long time. Hell, I don't think you even need to work anymore."

"Something feels off about this house," Mary said with a concerned look on her face.

"Don't, sweets. I know what you're thinking. It's all in your head. It's an old house and nothing more."

Mary shook her head and breathed in deeply, "I hope you're right."

Together, John and Mary followed their children inside the old house, which seemed more like a forgotten museum than a home. Dust lay thick on every surface, and each room they entered was a testament to a past abruptly left behind. Emma and Ben scampered excitedly from one shadowy corner to another, unearthing relics of the former inhabitants—old furniture draped in ghostly sheets of dust, and toys scattered as if the children who once played with them had vanished mid-game.

John watched with a growing sense of possibility, imagining the space brought back to life, its old charm restored. However, Mary appeared less convinced, her brow furrowed as she trailed her fingers over a dusty mantle.

"It looks like whoever lived here left in a hurry. Why would they leave all their belongings like that?" she asked, her voice tinged with unease.

John glanced around at the suspended history surrounding them, then offered a wry smile to lighten the mood. "Maybe they just decided they'd rather live in a cramped condo in the city," he joked, trying to spark a bit of humor in their exploration.

Mary gave him a weak smile, but her eyes still scanned the room warily, as if she expected the walls to start whispering secrets. "It's just odd, don't you think? All of this. ..abandoned. Makes you wonder what happened here."

John nodded, understanding her concerns but optimistic about the future. "We'll make it our own. Whatever happened before, this is our start. A little bit of mystery might just make it more interesting, right?"

John wrapped his arm around Mary, leading her playfully towards the next room of their new home. He wanted her to see the possibilities, not just the shadows of its past. With a mischievous grin, he stomped on the hardwood floor and looked back at her. "Check this out—these floors are solid! You can't even find planks this wide anymore."

Mary laughed and rolled her eyes, her smile brightening the dim room. "Just be careful, John. These floors might be all that's keeping the house from falling apart. Don't shake it down on our first day!"

After a few hours of exploration, the sound of a large truck rumbling up the driveway signaled the arrival of the moving van. John went outside to greet the movers, leaving Mary to continue her inspection of the house.

As the movers began unloading their belongings, John couldn't help but overhear snippets of their conversation.

"Yeah, I heard the last family that lived here just up and disappeared," one mover said, his voice low and conspiratorial.

"Seriously? That's creepy," another replied. "You think it's true?"

"Who knows, man. But it makes you wonder."

John's ears perked up at the mention of the house's past occupants. Disappeared? He hadn't heard anything about that. As he watched the movers work, he whispered to himself, "The real estate agent didn't say anything about people disappearing."

The afternoon sun spilled golden light across the Harper family's new front yard as the last boxes were hauled off the moving van. The house, an old structure with peeling paint and creaky floorboards, held a charm that only years and memories could bestow. As John and Mary divided the tasks of breathing life into their new home, John took charge of the living room, arranging furniture and sorting through boxes, while Mary set herself up in the kitchen, organizing pots and pans and setting up appliances in an attempt to infuse warmth into the heart of the house.

Upstairs, Emma and Ben found themselves standing in the hallway, each poised at the entrance to their new rooms. Emma, with her high school years towering over her like the tall, narrow doorway she leaned against, flipped her long hair over her shoulder and surveyed her domain with a mix of disdain and excitement. This space was hers alone—no more sharing with her little brother, whose boundless energy and relentless imagination often invaded her world of music and friends.

Ben, on the other hand, darted into his room with the uncontained enthusiasm typical of a fourth grader. His mind raced with possibilities as he explored each corner, already imagining where his collection of action figures and comic books would go. His room was a blank canvas for his adventures, a hiding spot for imaginary friends or foes.

"Hey, Ben, check this out!" Emma called from her doorway; her voice tinged with a rare excitement that caught

Ben's attention. He paused, a plastic superhero frozen in mid-leap in his hand, and looked up to see his sister waving him over.

Ben scampered across the hall to her room, where Emma pointed at an old, built-in shelf. "This could be perfect for your toy soldiers, you know. They can have their battles here, and then maybe we won't step on them all the time," she teased gently, a smile breaking through her usual too-cool facade.

Ben's eyes lit up; his earlier adventures forgotten. "Can they really stay here, Emma? In your room?" he asked, his voice filled with hope and a bit of disbelief.

"Sure," Emma shrugged, her affection for her little brother overshadowing her usual teenage aloofness. "But only if you keep them in order, General Ben," she added with a mock-serious tone, granting him not only space in her room but also a bit of her growing independence.

As Emma helped Ben set up his miniature army on the shelf, their laughter and chatter drifted downstairs, mingling with the sounds of John pushing furniture across the floor and Mary's soft humming from the kitchen. This house, with all its quirks and creaks, was beginning to feel like home.

It's So Cold

As the sun began to set. John stepped outside to take a break. He stood on the porch, gazing out at the ten acres that surrounded their new home. The vastness of the land was both exhilarating and daunting, bordered by endless acres of wilderness.

Mary joined him, wrapping her arms around herself against the evening chill. "Do you think we made the right decision?"

He took her hand in his, squeezing it gently. "I do, honey. This place, it's got potential. We'll make it work. We have to."

The first day in their new home ended with a quiet dinner around an old wooden table, the family finding solace in each other's company. The house, though in need of repair, held a promise of new beginnings. For now, John chose to ignore the whispered rumors and focus on the future, unaware of the dark history that the property held.

The first night in the new house passed uneventfully, the family was exhausted from their move and too tired to notice anything amiss. As dawn broke, the Harpers awoke to a bright, sunny morning. The house, now filled with their belongings, felt a little more like home.

John stretched and yawned as he made his way to the kitchen, the smell of freshly brewed coffee wafting through the air. Mary was already up, unpacking dishes and arranging them in the cupboards. "Good morning," he said, planting a kiss on her cheek. "How'd you sleep?"

"Better than I expected," Mary said, but there was a slight edge to her voice that made John look up from what he was doing. "It was quiet last night. Too quiet. I mean, not a cricket, no owls... nothing at all. That's weird for the country, right?" She glanced out the window as if half-expecting some woodland creature to prove her wrong. "Back up north, my nights were never this silent—always had owls hooting, frogs croaking, even coyotes howling. Doesn't it seem strange to you, this silence?"

John shrugged, trying to reassure her. "Maybe we're just not used to it yet. I'm sure it'll feel more normal in a few days."

The kids came bounding down the stairs, full of energy and excitement. "Can we go explore outside?" Ben asked, his eyes wide with anticipation.

"Sure," John said, ruffling his son's hair. "Just stay within sight of the house, okay?"

Emma rolled her eyes but followed her brother outside, the two of them eager to see what adventures awaited them on their ten-acre playground.

With the kids occupied, John and Mary returned to their tasks. John focused on setting up the living room and what would eventually become his home office.

"Sweetheart, we're going to need to call someone to get internet out here. I don't see anywhere to hook a router to."

"Did you check to see if this place can even get internet? I can't even get a phone signal out here."

John looked at Mary thoughtfully, concern evident in his voice. "I'm sure we can figure something out. When we head into town, I'll ask around. Maybe you can explore some of the local shops, and see if they're hiring. We did well selling the condo, but I know you won't like sitting around here all day. Plus, it would be a good way to get in with the locals.

Mary nodded as she continued organizing the kitchen, her tone optimistic. "Sounds like a plan. I'm sure I'll find something eventually."

A slight pause followed before she turned back to John with a playful smirk. "I kinda like when you told me that I wouldn't need to work anymore."

John chuckled, running a hand through his hair. "Well, if I land a decent teaching job after the summer, you definitely won't need to. But just in case, you know?"

Mary laughed, the tension easing between them. "I'm just teasing. Honestly, I'd love to work at a local shop. Small-town shops have their charm, don't they?" She gazed out the window, imagining the quaint storefronts of their new town. "I can see it now: me, running a little shop, swapping stories with the locals. It could be fun, right?"

John smiled, relieved to see her spirits lifted. "Sounds perfect. Let's make that happen."

Mary continued unpacking in the kitchen. As she worked, she couldn't shake the feeling that something was off. The house felt unusually cold, even though the sun was shining brightly outside. She shivered and pulled her sweater tighter around her.

In the living room, John was sorting through boxes when he heard Mary call out to him. "Hey, do you feel that? It's freezing in here."

John frowned and walked over to the thermometer that hung on the wall near the entryway and checked the level of the mercury. "The thermometer says it's 75 degrees. It must just be your imagination."

Mary nodded, though she didn't seem convinced. "Maybe. It's just... odd."

As the morning wore on, the kids' laughter drifted in through the open windows, a comforting sound amidst the unease Mary felt. Outside, Emma and Ben explored the overgrown garden and the edge of the dense forest that bordered their property.

"Look at this, Emma!" Ben shouted, pointing to an old, rusted swing set half-hidden by tall grass.

Emma approached; her curiosity piqued. "This must have been here for years. Think it still works?"

Ben gave it an experimental push, and the swing creaked ominously. "Seems sturdy enough. You want a turn?"

Emma hesitated, then shook her head. "You go first. It looks like a pile of Tetanus to me."

"What's Tetanus?" Ben asked as he looked at his sister, his face halfcocked to the side.

"Oh, never mind. Just be careful."

Even though her father had been out of the service for a few years, Emma was still very much like a mother figure to her little brother and would watch over him constantly.

As Ben clambered onto the swing, Emma wandered toward the tree line, feeling a strange pull toward the dense woods. She stopped at the edge, peering into the shadows. The forest was thick and dark, the trees seemingly endless.

Back in the house, Mary paused to catch her breath, wiping sweat from her forehead despite the persistent chill in the air. She glanced out the window and saw Emma standing at the edge of the forest. A sudden sense of foreboding washed over her. Her stomach twisted into knots as a cold dread settled deep within her bones,

As late afternoon light filtered through the windows, John and Mary busied themselves with the tasks of settling into their new home. John, a tall man with a broad frame honed from years of military discipline, methodically assembled the living room furniture. His steady hands, which once navigated the complexities of military operations as a Marine, now worked with equal precision on the nuts and bolts of their household fixtures.

Mary, her long hair pulled back into a neat ponytail, busied herself unpacking boxes in the kitchen. Raised in the quieter parts of Northern California, she had experienced the hustle of city life when her parents moved in search of work. At eighteen, while her parents settled back into the small-town life of Ukiah, Mary stayed behind for college, attending Cal State East Bay to earn her finance degree.

As they arranged the living room, Mary paused, a small smile breaking through as she glanced at John. "Do you remember the day we met? In that little boutique in San Francisco?" she asked, momentarily distracted from the eerie silence of their new home.

John chuckled, setting down a box of books. "How could I forget? I walked in, completely clueless about what to buy. There you were like you belonged in one of those cheerful movie scenes. You saved me from buying something utterly disastrous."

Mary laughed, the sound echoing softly in the quiet room. "You were so earnest about finding the perfect gift. I thought it was sweet. You just came back from Iraq, didn't you? The way you talked about wanting something genuine to remember home... it struck a chord with me."

John nodded, moving closer to her. "Yeah, that tour was rough. Coming back, I just wanted something... normal, I guess. You helped me find that normalcy again. And well, you gave me a lot more than just gift advice."

Sitting down beside her, John took her hand. "That day turned into coffee, then dinner, and suddenly I couldn't imagine not having you around. You brought a sense of peace I hadn't felt in a long time."

Mary squeezed his hand, her eyes meeting his. "And here we are, embarking on a whole new chapter. Though, admittedly, it's a bit more adventurous than I expected."

John's eyes softened as he looked around their shadow-filled home, then back at Mary before going back to moving boxes and Mary walked over and looked out the window. "We've faced challenges before, haven't we? We'll handle this one too. Together."

Their shared reminiscence brought a brief respite, a reminder of their deep bond formed in the most ordinary of moments—a bond they'd now rely on more than ever as they faced the mysteries of their new home.

Despite her usually upbeat demeanor, Mary couldn't shake a lingering unease as she looked out the kitchen window into the dense woods surrounding their new home. It felt too quiet, unnaturally so.

John noticed her distant gaze and paused his work, wiping his hands on a cloth as he walked over. His presence was reassuring, a solid certainty in the fluid world Mary sometimes found overwhelming. "It's probably just the time of year," he suggested, following her gaze into the thickening shadows. "Give it time. Maybe the animals are different over here. Maybe they're just being cautious with their new neighbors."

Mary tried to smile, appreciating his attempt to comfort her. "I hope you're right," she replied, her voice carrying a note of uncertainty that she rarely let show.

As the day wore on, Emma and Ben burst through the front door, breaking the eerie quiet with the news of their explorations. Ben's eyes sparkled with the vivid imagination of a child who could turn the simplest surroundings into an adventure. "We found an old swing set and some cool trails in the woods!" he announced, his enthusiasm painting a stark contrast to the somber moods of his parents.

"Sounds like you had a great time," John replied with a warm, encouraging smile, his rugged face softening. "Why don't you two wash up for dinner?"

THE CALLING

L ater that evening they gathered around the dinner
table, the house slowly filling with the comforting
smells of Mary's cooking—a skill she had honed as a nurturing counterbalance to the stress of her earlier career.
Mary's efforts to create a calming atmosphere were profound, especially in how she arranged their evening meals
to bring everyone together, a ritual that grounded them as
a family.

As they ate, Mary's eyes were repeatedly drawn to the
window, watching as the sunlight retreated and the shadows deepened around their secluded home. The silence
of the woods seemed to press against the glass, a blatant
contradiction to the lively conversation at the table. She
took a deep breath, reminding herself of the peace they had
come here to find.

"We made this move to find peace," she murmured more to herself than to anyone else, her voice almost lost in the clatter of plates and the children's animated chatter about their day. Determined, she focused back on the family, on Emma's gentle teasing of Ben and John's hearty laugh, the sounds forming a protective bubble against her fears.

This was their new beginning, Mary reminded herself, and she was determined to make it work. Her determination was a quiet force, much like the calm she had found in leaving the frenetic pace of finance behind—a testimony to her enduring belief that happiness was crafted from the simple moments spent with loved ones.

As they neared the end of their meal, Ben's brow furrowed in thought, his earlier excitement dimming into curiosity. "It's weird, though. I didn't see any animals around. Not even any birdies," he commented, pushing his plate aside.

"Maybe we just need to call them," he added with the earnestness only a child harboring dreams of being the king of the forest could possess. With a sudden burst of energy, he hopped off his chair and scampered to the front porch, ready to summon his woodland subjects.

Outside, under the blanket of twilight, Ben puffed up his chest and began whistling into the darkness, his notes hopeful and inviting, trying to communicate peace to any creature that was listening.

Back inside, Emma couldn't help but burst into laughter, overhearing her brother's attempts. She leaned against the kitchen doorway, amusement twinkling in her eyes. "You can't just call birds, you dork. Plus, it's nighttime. You need to do that in the morning. That's when birds come out. Haven't you heard the phrase, 'the early bird gets the worm?'"

Ben turned around, a puzzled look crossing his features. "No, I haven't, but that's a great idea! Maybe if I get some worms, I can really feed the birdie friends," he mused, his imagination already running wild with the prospect of befriending the forest animals through acts of kindness.

Emma rolled her eyes playfully, stepping out onto the porch to join him. "You're such a goof. But, hey, if you want to be Dr. Doolittle, you might need to adjust your schedule. Birds aren't exactly night owls, you know."

"But wouldn't it be cool if they were?" Ben countered, his eyes lighting up with the fun of the debate. "Imagine if we could talk to owls, too. Then we could really be friends with all the night creatures!"

Emma laughed again, ruffling his hair affectionately. "Sure, buddy. We'll befriend all the animals. Owls, squirrels, maybe even a bear or two. But for now, let's stick to birds that wake up with the sun, okay?"

Ben nodded; his initial disappointment was replaced by a new plan. "Okay, but first thing tomorrow, I'm getting up early. I'll find some worms, and then I'll show you how a real king of the forest does it!"

"Deal," Emma agreed, her teasing tone softening to one of endearment as she watched her little brother's enthusiasm. "But just make sure you don't wake me up too early, King Ben. Remember, queens need their beauty sleep."

The two of them chuckled together, their laughter mingling with the whispers of the forest around them, the night not as silent as before. As they turned to go back inside, a faint rustle in the underbrush hinted that perhaps Ben's calls hadn't gone entirely unheard.

Ben dashed back into the house; his face flushed with excitement from the thrilling rustle he had just heard outside. He skidded into the dining room, where John and Mary were still clearing the table from dinner.

"Mom! Dad! My calls worked—I heard something in the bushes!" he exclaimed, barely able to contain his glee.

John, always ready with a quip, grinned and teased, "Great, now you've just called all the skunks in the forest to our doorstep."

Mary rolled her eyes at John's jest, a familiar dance between them. "Stop it," she said with a mock sternness that only made his smile widen.

Undeterred, John leaned back in his chair, his eyes twinkling with mischief. "Or maybe it's the Appalachian leprechauns. They like to come out at night to rifle through your pockets and steal your change."

Mary shook her head, the corners of her mouth fighting a smile. "Enough, enough, you're going to give the kids nightmares."

John looked up, feigning innocence. "Oh, come on, honey, they know I'm joking."

Ben's eyes widened at the mention of leprechauns, his mind already spinning with the possibilities. "Maybe I can trap one and he can lead me to his pot of gold," he mused aloud, the gears turning in his head as he imagined outsmarting a leprechaun.

Emma, who had followed Ben back inside, chuckled at her brother's latest adventure plan. "Yeah, and maybe I'll catch a fairy to do my homework," she quipped, enjoying the playful banter.

John and Mary exchanged amused glances, their initial reservations about the move melting away with their children's laughter filling the house. This was what they had hoped for—a fresh start and a place where their kids could dream big, even if those dreams included mythical forest creatures.

As the family settled down for the evening, the house felt a little warmer, the shadows a little friendlier, and the possibilities of their new life seemed as boundless as Ben's imagination.

As they settled in for bed, Mary whispered to John, "Did you notice how cold the house got again this evening?"

He wrapped his arms around her, pulling her close. "It's an old house, sweets. It probably just needs some time to warm up properly. It's a lot bigger than our tiny condo and you're probably just not used to the cool mountain air. We'll get used to it. Don't worry."

Mary nodded, closing her eyes and trying to believe his words. But as she drifted off to sleep, the silence seemed to grow louder, and the chill in the air felt more like a warning than a mere quirk of their new home.

THE SILENCE

T he next morning, the Harper family decided to venture into town for supplies. The drive into Micaville
was picturesque, with winding roads flanked by towering
trees and the distant sound of the North Toe River rushing
over rocks. As they approached the town, the dense forest
opened up to reveal a quaint, small community nestled in
the heart of the Appalachian Mountains.

Micaville was charmingly old-fashioned, its main street
lined with small shops and colorful storefronts. A folk-art
gallery showcased local artists' work, with whimsical
sculptures and vibrant paintings displayed in the window.
Next door, a pottery shop boasted hand-crafted wares,
each piece unique and brimming with character. The
scent of fresh bread wafted from a bakery down the street,
mingling with the crisp mountain air.

Mary looked over at her husband with a hint of excitement he had not seen since they moved to North Carolina all the way from California. "I'd love to work in one of these shops. They remind me of the boutiques from back home."

He looked back over at Mary with a smile, "I knew you'd say that. See, I told you it was meant to be. After we pick up some food, why don't you walk around and see if anyone is looking to hire? I'll take the kids and try to get some internet to our place."

Mary placed her hand on John's thigh and he put his hand on top of hers. She took a deep breath before turning towards the back seat where the kids were quietly taking in the scene. "This seems like it will be the perfect place to start our new lives."

Ben couldn't care less and just wanted to get back home so he could go play outside. Emma on the other hand scoffed at her mother's statement.

As the Harper family continued their journey toward the local general store, tension simmered beneath the surface of their excitement. Seated in the back, Emma's patience was wearing thin.

"Mom, I haven't seen any other kids around. Is there even anything to do here? I'm not going to turn into some little redneck like you were. If we can't get internet out at our house, I'm going to lose my shit," Emma blurted out, frustration coloring her words.

Mary's head whipped around, her usually gentle face tightening with disapproval. "Emma! Don't use language like that, especially not around Ben," she scolded sharply.

John, trying to keep the peace while navigating the road, glanced at Emma through the rearview mirror. "You know, you used to be quite the little adventurer yourself when you were younger. Always out exploring, getting dirty—kinda like a tomboy."

"Ugh, Dad, how old are you? Nobody uses that term anymore. It's so anachronistic," Emma retorted, rolling her eyes. "Plus, you were hardly around back then, so how would you know?"

John's expression softened, a touch of regret passing through his eyes. "Anachro—what? What does that even mean?"

"It means you're old, Dad. Ancient, practically. You belong in the age of dinosaurs," Emma shot back, a smirk playing on her lips despite her sharp words.

John chuckled, though the laughter didn't reach his eyes as it usually did. "Well, I may be old, and yes, I was deployed a lot, but I was there for you and Ben more than you remember. And who knows, maybe dinosaurs made great friends. I could have used a few of those."

Mary sighed, looking between her husband and daughter. "Let's try to keep the swearing down, okay? And remember, we're all doing our best to adjust here. Let's support each other."

Ben, who had been quietly absorbing the back and forth, finally piped up, "Can we try to get internet first so I can play some Roblox? Then maybe find some dinosaur friends?"

The light-hearted comment broke the tension, pulling smiles from everyone in the car. He nodded, meeting Mary's eyes in the rearview mirror. "We'll sort out the internet first, scout's honor. Then we'll work on finding those dinosaur ghosts, buddy."

As laughter filled the car, the initial strains of moving seemed to dissolve, replaced by a shared anticipation of the new life awaiting them, no matter how many modern—or prehistoric—challenges they might face.

John turned his head and eyes back on the road. He had many regrets for staying in the service for as long as he did and missing so much of their children's lives. He had joined the Marines in 2001 and was plunged straight into the war on terror after 9/11. He was working with the 877th Engineering Battalion when his vehicle was struck by an IED. For this, he received a purple heart. The only thing that kept him alive that day was the thought of his beautiful family back home.

John knew Emma resented him for leaving her to grow up too fast, but he also knew that he had a duty to fight for freedom. He wanted to say something to her but figured it would be best if he didn't start an argument right now.

He parked the car, and the family stepped out, taking in the sights and sounds of their new town. Ben pointed excitedly at a candy store; its window filled with jars of brightly colored sweets. Emma, still a bit sullen, couldn't help but be intrigued by the local bookstore, its shelves visible through the large front window.

"Let's grab some food and then find a hardware store," John said, trying to keep things moving. "We can explore more after."

They made their way down the street, stopping at a small café for breakfast. The cozy interior was filled with mismatched furniture and cheerful locals, who greeted them with friendly smiles. As they ate, John and Mary discussed the plans for fixing up the house, while the kids marveled at the homemade pastries and hot chocolate.

After their meal, the Harper family headed to the local J.R. Thomas General Store. The store was a charming relic, where the past and present mingled effortlessly. Wooden floors groaned softly under their steps, adding a rhythm to their entry, and shelves brimming with an eclectic mix of groceries and hardware items bore the weight of both dust and time. As they pushed through the old, paint-chipped door, a bell above tinkled a greeting, its sound as crisp as the autumn air outside.

The cashier, her gray-streaked hair framing her face, leaned closer to her companion, a whisper threading through her words tinged with a heavy southern drawl. "Them Harper descendants finally come home," she murmured, her eyes darting to ensure the newcomers couldn't hear. "Father's gonna be over the moon to have his own kin back, to take up his throne."

Her companion, an older man with deep-set eyes, nodded in agreement, his voice low and gravelly. "And maybe, just maybe, my girl can come home too," she added, a mix of hope and a darker intent flickering across her expression.

"We gotta make 'em feel welcome like they belong here with us," she continued, her whisper almost inaudible. "But I'll do whatever Father needs to keep 'em here. If it means my daughter can finally come back, I'll play along."

Ben, having edged closer under the pretense of selecting a candy, caught fragments of their hushed conversation. Words like "Harper," "Father," and "home" wove through the air, settling uneasily in his mind. Though he couldn't grasp the full meaning, the secretive tone and the mention of his family stirred a wary curiosity as he returned to his parents, the cashier's covert words echoing ominously in his young ears.

"Wow, this place is so cool!" Ben exclaimed, his voice echoing slightly in the high-ceilinged space, filled with the scent of aged wood and stain. His eyes darted from one interesting oddity to another, each item sparking another burst of curiosity.

Emma, however, wrinkled her nose as she surveyed the vintage setup. "It looks like a museum in here," she remarked her tone a mix of awe and skepticism. "How old is this place?"

"Emma, shush," Mary scolded gently, giving her a soft elbow nudge. "Be respectful."

The cashier chuckled, unfazed by the mixed reactions of the newcomers. "Older than you can imagine, dear. This store has been the heart of the town for generations. It's seen many faces and heard many stories." The man she was talking to waved to the Harpers and smiled as he walked out of the store. She then stood up, smoothing her apron. "Anything specific I can help you find today?"

John, always keen to explore without a plan, responded with a friendly shake of his head. "Oh, we're just here to look around today, thank you."

"Of course!" the cashier replied with an easy laugh. "Well, if you need any help or can't find what you're looking for, just give me a holler. And if we don't have it here, I can surely point you in the right direction."

As they ventured deeper into the store, the kids continued to marvel—Ben at the quaint charm of the historic establishment, and Emma slowly warming to its nostalgic allure, each creak of the floorboards telling a story of years gone by.

As the Harper family delved deeper into the aisles of the store, they were momentarily drawn back to the front as the cashier's voice, rich with a local drawl, carried warmly across the room. "Y'all just driving through?" she observed with a friendly nod.

John smiled and confirmed as they approached the counter again. "No, we just moved in. We're over in the old house up Route 80, near the North Toe River."

Her eyes lit up with recognition, her smile broadening, and trying to play it off as if she didn't already know who they were. "Oh, you're in the old Harper House! Beautiful area, but quite the fixer-upper. You folks have your work cut out for you. How are the kids settling in?"

Mary, with Emma and Ben trailing close behind, responded, her voice tinged with a blend of surprise and mild concern. "The Harper House? That's interesting—our last name is Harper too. What are the odds? Maybe John has some relatives up here we don't know about." She paused, then continued, "It's quite a shift from city life, but we're starting to find our way around, getting to know the area," her tone hopeful yet reflective as they navigated this new chapter.

The cashier smirked a little when she heard their last name, but she quickly masked it with a warm, friendly smile tinged with that thick Southern drawl. "Well now, that's an interesting coincidence. Legend has it an old man by the name of Harold Harper built that place back in the late 1800s. Folks around here say he was once the town mayor and known for throwin' some wild gatherings at his home. Unfortunately, a lot of our town's history got up and vanished in a big fire that swept through here in the 1920s. From what I've been told, his place was the only one left standin' after it all."

She leaned in a bit, lowering her voice as if sharing a town secret. "My daddy always said that Harold was a bit touched in the head, even went so far as to claim he was the one who started that fire. But, shoot, who really knows the truth of it all?"

The cashier leaned forward, resting her arms on the counter, her expression one of genuine interest. "Well, you've come to the right place if you need any pointers or just want to chat. Folks around here are always ready to lend a hand or share a story. Don't hesitate to stop by any time."

This friendly exchange, though brief, gave the Harpers a stronger sense of connection to their new community. The creaking floors beneath their feet and the welcoming chatter added another layer to their settling in.

"Just make sure you city slickers watch out for the Mica mines, especially your youngsters." The cashier added, before picking up the magazine that she had on the counter beside her.

John glanced at Mary, then back at the cashier. "Mica mines? I don't even know what those are. But the real estate agent did mention to be careful because there are a lot of open mineshafts around the area."

The cashier nodded; her expression thoughtful. "Mica mines have been around these parts for years. They used to mine the stuff back in the day. Those old shafts can be dangerous, so it's good to keep an eye on your kiddos."

Mary shivered slightly, the thought of open mineshafts adding to her unease about their new home. "Thanks for the warning. We'll definitely be careful."

As they picked up their supplies, the cashier continued to chat with them. "My name's Barbara, by the way. Lived here all my life."

"Nice to meet you, Barbara," John said, shaking her hand. "We're John and Mary Harper. These are our kids, Emma and Ben."

Barbara smiled warmly at the children. "Well, welcome to Micaville. It's a small town, but we've got a lot of history and some interesting folklore."

Mary, intrigued, leaned forward. "Folklore? Like what?"

Barbara glanced up, her gaze quickly sweeping the general store to ensure privacy before she leaned in closer. "That land you've moved onto was once a labor camp for miners. There's an eerie tale tied to the woods surrounding it. It's said that those who venture into the woods at night, or dare to whistle after dark... well, they often lose their minds." She paused, her voice lowering to a whisper, "They say it can let spirits into your home."

Mary's expression shifted from curiosity to concern. "Lose their minds? How exactly?"

With another cautious glance around, Barbara slowly drew a finger across her throat in a deliberate motion. "The legend goes that they'd end up taking their own lives. No one knows for sure why. Many of the older folks think it was just a story concocted to keep kids from wandering off and falling into the mineshafts after dark."

Barbara straightened up, her demeanor sobering. "But the tales persist that whistling after dark or simply setting foot in those woods can summon a dark force. Not the friendly type, mind you. I always say, 'If it ain't broke, don't fix it.' Though plenty of outsiders dismiss it as hogwash."

Emma, attempting to cut through the tension, raised an eyebrow skeptically. "Sounds like a great plot for a horror movie."

John, who had been half-listening while browsing a nearby shelf, chimed in with a raised eyebrow. "Spirits, huh? Sounds like the kind of story you tell around a campfire to spook kids."

Barbara gave a short laugh, though it lacked warmth. "Maybe so, dear. But around here, it's wise to heed such tales. They been around much longer than any of us."

The atmosphere thickened with the gravity of Barbara's words, casting a somber shadow over the Harper family's initial excitement.

Barbara shuffled her feet, a glint of mischief fading from her eyes as she sensed Mary's growing unease. She let out a nervous chuckle, scratching the back of her head. "Aw, shucks, I'm just pullin' your leg a bit, darlin'. We got our local tales, sure as the sky's blue, but we like to rib the newcomers a smidge. Ain't no harm meant, truly. Or... maybe there's a kernel of truth in 'em? Heh."

Mary's eyes narrowed slightly, the smile fading from her lips. "That's... a bit disconcerting. It sounds like you might be trying to soften the blow of something genuinely worrying."

Barbara gave a nonchalant shrug, her expression a mix of earnestness and evasion. "Well, I reckon I might sound like a crazy ol' hillbilly to y'all, but honestly, most folks 'round here, they don't take kindly to talkin' 'bout such things. It's part of our lore, sure, but it's best left alone. Just tread lightly, honey. Temptin' fate 'round these parts can be... well, let's just say it ain't recommended."

As Barbara's tales of the dark woods settled over the room, a sudden memory flashed through Mary's mind, casting a chill down her spine. She recalled the previous night when Ben, filled with youthful curiosity and oblivious to local superstitions, had playfully whistled into the shadowy embrace of the woods. The memory of that innocent sound, now tainted with ominous implications, made her heart skip a beat.

Mary glanced nervously at Emma, who seemed on the verge of sharing Ben's nocturnal adventure with Barbara. Catching her daughter's eye, Mary subtly shook her head, a silent plea etched in her worried expression. Emma paused, her lips pursing slightly as she caught her mother's unspoken message. With a slight nod, Emma redirected her attention, keeping the secret safely tucked away.

Mary breathed a quiet sigh of relief. She couldn't bear the thought of adding more fear to Ben's already rich imagination, especially with such a haunting suggestion that his innocent whistle could have stirred unseen forces. As the conversation flowed around her, Mary's mind remained partly anchored in that eerie moment, the sound of Ben's whistle echoing like a foreboding whisper against the crisp night air.

She wrapped her arms around herself, feeling suddenly cold, and resolved silently to keep a closer watch over the children's evening activities. The thought of those dark woods bordering their new home, potentially filled with unseen dangers, urged a protective instinct fiercely alive within her.

John tried to maintain a light-hearted tone. "Well, we'll be sure to keep our whistling to daylight hours then."

Barbara's chuckle was more audible this time. "You do that. And remember, if you need anything or have questions, come back here. In Micaville, we look out for our own."

John nodded his head and began to turn around but remembered they needed to find out how to get internet service to the old place.

"Hey Barbara, you wouldn't happen to know how I would go about getting internet to our house, would you?

"I'm not sure if they go out that far. I'll give Tony a call. He's our resident technician out here. If anyone knows about that stuff it'd be him. I'll send him out your way."

"Thanks, Barbara," John said as he turned back around and headed further into the store to finish up their shopping.

"Anytime honey," Barbara said before slapping her hand on the table and muttering to herself. Those damn city slickers and their internet.

Mary glanced at Barbara, who had already buried her nose in her magazine. With a gentle curiosity, she asked, "Barbara, if you don't mind me askin', do you have any children of your own?"

Barbara peeked over her magazine, pausing a bit too long before lowering it slowly. She seemed to weigh her words carefully. "I'm sorry, Barbara. You don't need to answer that if it's too personal," Mary quickly added, sensing her hesitation.

"Oh, it's alright, darlin'," Barbara responded with a faint smile. "I do have a little girl. Her name's Joann, and she'll be turnin' ten come next month. That girl's my whole world, truly."

Mary brightened at the mention. "Oh my! She's the same age as Ben. Maybe one day we could set up a playdate for them."

Barbara closed her eyes briefly, and Mary sensed a shadow pass over the conversation. "I reckon Joann would like that mighty fine," Barbara continued, her voice tinged with a hint of sadness, "but she's been poorly lately, real sick, you know."

Noticing Barbara's eyes begin to glisten with unshed tears, Mary decided not to delve any deeper. "Oh, the poor dear. Well, I hope she gets to feeling better soon. We can sort something out later, once she's up and about."

The conversation dipped into a thoughtful silence, each woman lost in her concerns, yet the air between them filled with a shared understanding.

The Harpers thanked Barbara and loaded their bags into the car. As they drove back to their new home, Mary couldn't shake the unease that had settled in the pit of her stomach.

"What do you think about what Barbara said?" she asked John.

John shrugged, trying to keep things light. "It's just folklore, Mary. Every town has its ghost stories. We'll be fine."

Mary nodded, but the sense of unease lingered. As they pulled into their driveway, the old house loomed ahead of them, its dark windows watching silently.

THE STORIES

With the groceries and supplies unloaded, the family got to work. John set up the paint supplies and began planning the first of many home improvement projects, while Mary sorted the groceries and started making lunch. The kids, still full of energy, played outside, their laughter echoing through the trees.

As the day wore on, the sense of unease Mary felt persisted. The house still felt too cold, and the silence of the surrounding forest seemed almost oppressive. She couldn't shake the feeling that something was watching them, lurking just out of sight.

But for now, they focused on the task at hand, determined to turn their new house into a home. As the sun began to set and the shadows lengthened once again, the warnings from Barbara echoed in Mary's mind. She tried to push them aside, focusing on the work ahead and the promise of a fresh start.

As evening fell, the Harper family gathered in the living room, exhausted but pleased with their progress. The house was starting to feel more like a home, with familiar items unpacked and placed around the rooms. They decided to take a break and watch a movie together, hoping to relax after a long day of work.

The old television they had brought from the city flickered to life, casting a warm glow in the dimly lit room. Ben curled up on the couch with a blanket, his tousled hair falling into his eyes. Emma sat cross-legged on the floor, still somewhat distant but drawn into the comfort of family time. John and Mary settled into their chairs, sharing a bowl of popcorn and exchanging relieved smiles.

Even with the volume of the T.V. turned up, the silence in the house was burrowing into Mary's head. It was as if she could sense something watching from right outside the house. All of a sudden there was a loud knock at the door forcing Mary to jump from her chair.

"Who is that? It's almost ten o'clock." Mary said with a frightened look on her face.

"I'm not sure. I'll go have a look." John said.

John walked over to the front door and Mary heard the door open with a loud creak.

"Who are you?" John said as he swung open the door.

"Name's Tony. Barbara sent me up to see if I could get you guys into the twenty-first century."

"Pretty late for a house call don't you think," He said, with a hint of doubt.

"Ya, I apologize. I usually don't make calls this late but since you're new in town I wanted to make a good first impression. I was just down the holler working your neighbor Zessie's house. The phone company just finished pulling a line up this way a few weeks ago and I've been busy getting everyone landlines and internet service. If it's okay I'd like to get you all set up tonight so I don't need to come out this way again. I got everything in my truck."

"That would be amazing," John said, his skepticism washing from his face.

"Hey honey, Tony is here and he's wondering if he can get us hooked up to the internet tonight?"

Emma, overhearing what her dad just said, looked over at her mom with a smile she had not seen since moving out into the woods. "Please, Mom. Please. I need to check my IG and I'm sure my friends are blowing me up on TikTok."

Mary agreed to let him in as if she had a choice. She got up from her chair and walked over to greet Tony, quickly fixing her hair to look more presentable for the unforeseen visitor.

"Hello ma'am, name's Tony. It's good to see someone finally move into this place. I thought it was just going to rot into the earth. I'm sure folks have been telling you about the local folklore. Don't believe any of that crap. I swear they do that to outsiders to try and get them to move away."

"Are you from around here Tony?" He asked hoping they had met another implant like themselves.

Nah. I'm from Texas originally. I came out here for a part-time gig helping run telephone lines about five years ago and just never left. Where are ya'll from?"

"We've moved out here from California," John said as he began to lead Tony to where the office was.

"Well, I'm glad ya'll made it out of that shit hole. Excuse my French." Tony said as he looked over to see Mary standing next to Emma and Ben.

"How old are the little ones."

"Well, Ben just turned ten, and Emma over there is about to be sixteen going on twenty-six."

Tony began laughing hysterically, "They sure do grow up quick."

"Jesus, tell me about it. Any kids of your own, Tony," John asked as he joined in on the laughter.

"I only have... or had the one. She'd be thirteen." Tony said as he abruptly stopped laughing.

Mary took a few steps towards John and Tony before speaking with a hint of sadness. "Oh my. I'm so sorry. I hope you don't mind me asking, but what happened."

Tony adjusted his cap, a flicker of pain crossing his face before he masked it with a practiced smile. "Ah, it's been tough, you know. My daughter—she's been gone a few years now. I suspect she might have run off to be with her mother after the divorce. It hit her hard, and she started wandering off into the mountains, talking about joining 'them' to protect me. Then one day, she just didn't come back. The only thing that was missing from her room was an old Raggedy Ann doll that she'd carry everywhere with her."

He sighed heavily; his gaze distant. "We scoured the hills for months but found nothing. I even tried to reach out to her mom, but she's vanished too, changed her number and all. Some of the locals—they've told me they've seen her around, snagging food left out on porches and still carrying her favorite doll around with her. They say she's not alone, runs with Barbara's girl, who's also missing. They're convinced both kids are up to no good, part of some old family curse they say ties back to Barbara's ancestors."

Tony shook his head, a wry smile curling his lips. "I don't buy into the local superstitions, though. This place has a way of making people believe all sorts of wild tales. Anyway, let's focus on getting you folks settled in, and get that internet running. I bet Emma's eager to hop online, huh?" His tone lightened, trying to steer the conversation away from the darker threads.

Tony spent the next few hours running lines from the main telephone terminal out front, through the basement, and into the rooms. When he was all finished, they had a solid WIFI connection and a new landline.

John shook his hand with a firm grip, "Well what's the damage?"

"You guys don't owe me anything. Think of it as a welcome gift."

"Well, can we at least buy you lunch next time we're in town?"

"Of course. Give me a call anytime you need something. Tony said as he pulled a piece of scratch paper and pen from his front pocket and wrote down his number. "This is my cell number. Feel free to call day or night."

"Thanks, Tony. It was nice to meet you and hope we see you soon." Mary said as she sat back in her chair grabbing a handful of popcorn.

Tony headed for the front door before turning around one last time. "You folks have a nice evening now. Sorry, I interrupted your movie. Remember what I said, don't listen to the locals about the crazy stories. They are just trying to rattle ya'll."

"All right Tony, you have a nice evening as well," John said before closing the door behind him.

The four of them finished the movie. John yawned and stretched. "All right, time for bed, everyone. We've got another busy day tomorrow. And Emma, wait until tomorrow to catch up with your friends, it's already past midnight."

Emma rolled her eyes, "okay dad."

The kids groaned but didn't protest, too tired to argue. They headed upstairs, and soon the house was quiet once again. Mary followed John into their bedroom, still trying to ignore the strange feeling that had settled over her.

As she changed into her pajamas, the weight of the cashier's words hung heavily in the air. "John, do you think we should tell the kids about what Barbara said? About not whistling after dark?" she asked, her voice tinged with concern.

John, who was getting ready for bed himself, was quick to dismiss her worries. "No, Mary. I don't want to scare them with local bullshit stories. They're already adjusting to a lot of new things. Let's not add to it," he replied firmly, shaking his head as he tossed his shirt into the laundry.

Mary let out a heavy sigh, the fabric of her pajama top rustling softly in the stillness of the room. "I suppose you're right. It's just... unsettling," she admitted, folding her arms tightly across her chest. "Today, I asked Barbara if she had any children, and she told me about her daughter, Joann. I mentioned setting up a playdate, and she said Joann was sick. But now, Tony is telling us that his kid is missing, and apparently, so is Joann. Something's not adding up here, John. I'm telling you, something is definitely off."

John stepped closer and wrapped his arms around her, pulling her into a reassuring embrace. "It's just folklore, Mary. Remember what Tony said? The locals love to spin these tales to scare away outsiders. And it seems to be working," he said with a soft chuckle, trying to lighten the mood.

Mary, however, wasn't easily swayed. She pulled back slightly to look at him, her expression serious. "It's not just my imagination, John. When I lived on Mountain House Road, I saw things. I heard things that weren't normal, and I wasn't the only one. Barbara might be exaggerating, but I believe there's some truth to what she says. I have the same eerie feeling here that I did when I was younger. Something just doesn't feel right, and I think Ben might have accidentally invited them into our house."

John's expression shifted from comforting to slightly frustrated. "Come on. Do you really think something as simple as whistling can summon Casper the friendly ghost into our home?"

"Spirits, John. Not ghosts. And yes, I do think it's possible. The spirits—or whatever they are—might not want us here, just like some of the locals," Mary countered, her voice firm.

Trying to inject some humor into the situation, John offered a playful smirk. "Okay, honey. How about tomorrow I call up the Ghostbusters, and they can come over with their proton packs to suck up all the little devils?"

Mary didn't crack a smile. "I'm being serious, John. If strange things start happening around here, I'm not sticking around. You can stay here and make friends with them if you want."

John's face softened, recognizing the genuine fear in her eyes. "We'll be just fine, sweetheart. Let's try to get some sleep, okay? I promise, that once we settle in, all these creepy feelings will start to fade. You'll see," he reassured her, his voice gentle.

Mary nodded slowly, unconvinced but exhausted. "I hope you're right," she whispered as they climbed into bed, the shadows of the night pressing against the windows, silent witnesses to their disquiet.

As Mary finally succumbed to sleep, her mind descended into a shadowy world woven from the day's unsettling conversations. She found herself wandering through a dense, dark forest under a moonless sky. The air was thick with mist that clung to her skin, making each step feel heavy and labored. The trees loomed ominously, their branches clawing at the sky like skeletal hands.

A chilling breeze whispered through the undergrowth, carrying with it faint voices that seemed to curl around her, drawing closer with each gust. "Mary..." the voices called, elongating her name into a sinister hiss. The temperature dropped sharply, wrapping her in a cloak of cold that seeped deep into her bones.

She tried to move, to escape the eerie chorus, but her feet were rooted to the spot as if the forest itself held her captive. The whispering intensified, becoming a cacophony of murmurs. Then, cutting through the noise, a clear, chilling voice spoke directly into her ear, "Thank you for letting us in."

The words struck her with a terror so profound that her breath caught in her throat. She felt an overwhelming presence around her, as though invisible beings were closing in, their coldness a tangible force threatening to consume her. The forest seemed to pulse with a wicked energy; the darkness was not just a lack of light but a living, breathing entity.

Desperately, Mary tried to scream, to call out for John, for anyone. But her voice was swallowed by the oppressive silence that now blanketed the woods. The chilling realization dawned on her that she was utterly alone, trapped in this nightmare landscape with no apparent escape.

As the cold tightened its grip, a profound sadness washed over her, mingling with her fear. It was as if the forest mourned its corruption, lamenting the darkness that had seeped into its roots. This sorrow, however, provided no comfort—it only deepened her sense of dread, for it spoke of old, irreversible curses and the inevitable spread of shadow.

THE NIGHTMARES

S uddenly, she awoke with a jolt, her body shooting upright in bed. Her heart pounded fiercely against her ribcage, and she could still feel the residual cold clinging to her skin. The room was silent, but it took her several moments to convince herself that she was indeed back in the safety of her bedroom and not lost in the haunted woods of her nightmare. Sweat beaded her forehead, and she shivered, not just from the dream but from the eerie echo of gratitude that seemed to linger in the air.

Despite the chilling nightmare that had disrupted her sleep, Mary's fear was quickly dispelled as the morning light crept through the curtains. Her anxiety melted away when Ben and Emma burst into the room, their faces alight with the excitement of a new day. They clambered onto the bed, their laughter and energy infectious as they snuggled up close to her.

Feeling the comforting weight of her children beside her, Mary's heartbeat steadied. The terror of the night's dream receded, pushed to the back of her mind as the reality of her family's warmth enveloped her. She exchanged a look with John, who had watched the kids' joyful entrance, and a silent agreement passed between them.

With renewed determination, they decided to focus on the day ahead. Mary and John resumed their efforts to make the old house a home, channeling their energy into renovations and decorations. Together, they worked, transforming the space, piece by piece, into a reflection of their family's spirit and love.

Emma and Ben, eager to continue their exploration, finished breakfast in record time and dashed outside, promising to stay within sight of the house. John and Mary were engrossed in unpacking and cleaning, the rhythmic tasks providing a welcome distraction from her lingering uneasiness.

As the day wore on, subtle oddities began to surface. Mary noticed that certain rooms seemed colder than others, even though they were on the same floor. She also found old, faded photographs tucked away in a drawer, images of people she didn't recognize standing in front of their house, their expressions somber as if they knew it would be the last photo they would take as a family.

John, meanwhile, discovered an old trapdoor on the living room floor. He called Mary over, and together, they managed to pry it open, revealing a narrow staircase leading down into darkness.

"Should we check it out?" Mary asked, peering into the black void below.

"Might as well. It could be useful storage space."

John and Mary each clutched a flashlight as they descended the creaking stairs into the basement, the beams from their lights cutting through the overwhelming darkness. The air grew cooler and damper with each step, hinting at the seldom-visited space below their new home. As they reached the bottom, the basement opened up into a surprisingly spacious area. The stone walls, cold and unyielding, were paired with wood-planked floors that added a creaking chorus to their cautious steps.

Their flashlights swept across the room, revealing old crates and dusty shelves that seemed to sag under the weight of long-forgotten belongings. Cobwebs stretched from corner to corner, dancing lightly in the air stirred up by their movement.

Mary wrapped her arms around herself, feeling the chill seep deeper into her bones. "I don't like this babe. It feels... wrong somehow." Her voice echoed slightly, amplifying the unnerving atmosphere.

John, ever the pragmatist, tried to lighten the mood as he walked a bit further into the shadowy room. He stomped his foot down on a section of the flooring where the wood appeared slightly peeled up. The resonating sound it produced echoed oddly in the enclosed space.

"Do you hear that, Mary? It sounds like there's something hollow beneath here. I wonder what's underneath these planks."

Mary took a step back, her discomfort growing. "I don't know, and honestly, I don't really want to find out right now. Let's just go back upstairs and check on the kids," she suggested, her voice tense.

He paused, considering her apprehension, then wrapped an arm around her shoulders in a comforting gesture. "Let's just give it a quick once-over and head back up, okay? I'm sure it's nothing. And you know Emma—she's like a second mom to Ben. They'll be fine for a few more minutes."

He smiled, trying to reassure her, his confidence buoyed by the thought of their daughter's maturity and nurturing nature. "Let's just see if there's anything else down here worth noting. We'll clean it up, and make it part of the home. It'll be fine."

Reluctantly, Mary nodded, allowing the light from John's flashlight to guide them further into the basement's mysteries. Despite her unease, she trusted her loving husbands judgment, but the oppressive feel of the basement lingered, making her all the more eager to return to the light and laughter of their children upstairs.

As they moved further into the basement, the faint sound of whistling echoed through the dark, a haunting melody that sent chills down Mary's spine.

"Did you hear that?" Mary whispered; her eyes wide with fear.

He frowned, straining to listen, but he could not hear anything but the squeaky floorboards. "It's probably just the wind moving through the cracks in the house."

Mary shook her head, gripping his arm tightly. "It sounded like someone whistling."

John tried to reassure her, though he knew she was lost in her world of ghosts and goblins. "It's an old house. It's probably just the wind. Come on, let's head back upstairs."

They quickly retreated from the basement, the eerie sound echoing in her mind. Back in the living room, Mary was haunted by the notion that they had disturbed something best left untouched.

That evening, as the family gathered for dinner, the atmosphere felt heavier. Mary couldn't help but glance out the window, her thoughts returning to the strange whistling in the basement.

After dinner, the family settled in for what they hoped would be a peaceful evening. Mary tried to set aside her lingering concerns, concentrating on the warmth of her family and the coziness of their new home. However, as the shadows deepened and the house fell into profound silence, her sense of unease crept back, more intense than before.

Emma and Ben, thrilled to finally have internet access, retreated to their rooms, eager to reconnect with friends. John, exhausted from the day's activities, decided to turn in early, his thoughts untroubled by the worries that nagged at Mary. Alone with her apprehensions, Mary found herself listening to the stillness, her anxiety growing as the night wore on.

In the distance, an owl hooted, its call echoing through the night. Mary listened intently, waiting for any other sounds to break the silence. But none came, and the oppressive quiet of the country seeped into her every pore, making her skin feel as though it was on fire. It was almost as if the owl was trying to warn her of something. Trying to tell her to leave while they still had the chance.

As Mary lay in bed, her gaze fixed on the ceiling, Barbara's ominous words echoed in her mind. The local legends, filled with tales of shadows and unseen presences, seemed to weave their way through her thoughts. She drew in a deep breath, trying to dismiss the creeping dread as mere folklore, yet the chill of unease was hard to ignore.

As the house settled into the deep silence of the night, Mary tossed and turned in her bed, her mind unable to let go of the strange whistling she had heard earlier. The air felt heavy, pressing down on her chest, making it hard to breathe. She finally drifted off into a restless sleep, her dreams vivid and unsettling.

THEY'RE SO REAL

In her dream, Mary once again found herself at the edge of the ominous forest that skirted their property. Trees towered above, branches intertwining to obscure the moon, casting deep shadows across the forest floor. Mist wound its way around the tree trunks, seeming to move with purpose, chilling the night air.

Her heart thudded loudly as she spotted Emma and Ben ahead, their small figures dwarfed by the imposing woods. "Emma! Ben!" she shouted, but the fog seemed to swallow her cries, muffling the sound until it was barely a breath.

The children turned to her, their faces unnaturally pale and blank, as if they were no longer themselves. From the deeper shadows, a shape stirred—a dark figure that seemed to shift and change as she watched. It hovered near her children, watching them with an unsettling focus.

The figure issued a series of low, guttural tones that resonated through the still air. The sound wrapped around the children, drawing them closer. Emma and Ben moved as if in a trance, each step deliberate, heading toward the figure that seemed both part of the shadows and apart from them.

"No! Stay away from there!" Mary tried to scream, but her voice came out as a faint whisper, powerless in the overwhelming quiet of the forest. Emma and Ben continued their slow, mesmerized walk towards the figure.

In a panic, Mary attempted to run towards them, her feet heavy against the damp earth. Each step felt like wading through mud, her movements sluggish and strained. She watched in horror as the figure extended what looked like a hand toward Ben, its fingers elongated and twitching unnaturally.

As she finally broke through the invisible barrier holding her back, she reached out to grab Emma, pulling her back sharply. The figure's hand brushed against Ben's arm, leaving a dark stain that spread rapidly like ink across his sleeve. Ben turned his head slowly towards Mary, his eyes hollow, as if the light within him had been extinguished.

Fighting against the dread that clawed at her insides, Mary yanked Emma back towards the house, glancing over her shoulder to see the dark figure retreating into the mist with Ben, who now moved with the same eerie purpose as his captor.

Mary awoke with a start, her heart racing and her body drenched in sweat. She sat up, clutching the covers, and glanced over at John, who was sleeping soundly beside her. She wanted to wake him, to tell him about the dream, but she hesitated. He had dismissed her fears before, and she didn't want to seem irrational.

John lay in bed, his eyes closed but his mind alert. He too had dreamt of the forest, but in his dream, he had been the one standing at the edge, watching as the dark figure lurked among the trees. It had felt as though the shadow was aware of him, as though it had turned its gaze towards him with a silent promise of something terrible to come.

John shook off the feeling, not wanting to feed into Mary's growing hysteria. Since he had returned from overseas, he had flashbacks and nightmares almost every night, so this was nothing new to him. He figured out a long time ago that if he gave them too much weight, he'd drive himself crazy. Mary on the other hand had always been an emotional person and he worried that she might start to take all of this too seriously. He turned over, trying to find a comfortable position, but sleep eluded him.

It was only six in the morning, but Mary couldn't go back to sleep and the kids were already up. Mary's exhaustion was evident in the dark circles under her eyes and the way she moved through the house with a sluggish determination. She busied herself in the kitchen, trying to shake off the remnants of her nightmare. The children seemed oblivious to her anxiety, chattering excitedly about their plans to explore more of the property.

"Mom, can we check out the forest today?" Ben asked, his eyes bright with anticipation.

Mary hesitated, her mind flashing back to the dream. "Just be careful," she said finally, her voice tight. "And don't go too far."

Emma rolled her eyes. "We're not babies, Mom. We know how to be careful."

John overheard the kid's plans and came in to talk to them before they ran out the door. "There are open mine shafts on the property, so you need to be very careful. Do you understand me?"

"What's a mineshaft, Dad?" Ben said with a confused look on his face.

"You really don't know what a mineshaft is, you're such a dork?" Emma said with a typical teenage attitude.

"It's okay. Ben doesn't watch YouTube all day long like you do. Ben, they used to dig really deep holes around here to look for different minerals. When they were done digging the holes they never covered them up and if you accidentally fall into one you could get hurt really bad, or worse. So just be careful where you walk out there."

"Mineshaft, okay, gotcha Dad. We'll be careful."

The children grabbed their jackets and ran outside, their laughter echoing through the yard. Mary watched them go; her heart heavy with worry.

John found her standing by the window, her hands clenched into fists. He wrapped an arm around her shoulders. "Hey, what's wrong?"

She leaned into his embrace, grateful for his presence. "I had a dream last night. It was... unsettling. Something in the forest was watching the kids, inviting them to go deeper."

He leaned in and kissed the top of her head. "I had a similar dream. But it's just that—a dream. Let's not get carried away with this."

Mary looked up at him, searching his face for reassurance. "What if it's not just a dream? What if there's something out there?"

John sighed. "Let's take it one step at a time. It's probably because we're in a new place and we've been hearing a lot about the urban legends around here. We'll keep an eye on the kids and make sure they stay close. But you can't let this fear you have control you. I got an idea to cheer you up."

John strolled over to the radio and connected his phone to the receiver. He selected "Good Riddance" by Green Day, the very song that had played during their first dance as newlyweds. Turning back to Mary, he extended his hands in invitation. With a playful smirk and a shake of her head, Mary couldn't resist. It had been thirteen years since their wedding, yet the steps came back to them effortlessly. As they danced, Mary's swirling worries began to fade, and a sigh of relief escaped her as she rested her head on John's shoulder, enveloped in the comfort of their shared memory. After the song was over John went back to painting while Mary decided to help out by painting all the trim around the windows.

The day passed slowly, each creak of the house and the rustle of the leaves outside heightening the tension. Mary couldn't shake the feeling of being watched, her eyes constantly darting to the windows as she worked.

John busied himself with renovations around the house, channeling his energy into tangible improvements to push away the creeping unease that seemed to have settled over Mary. He painted the walls a fresh, cheerful color, tightened creaky floorboards, and began to tackle the cluttered basement. Despite these distractions, the eerie whistle from the basement the day before haunted the edges of his thoughts, a persistent reminder of the unsettling stories they'd heard since arriving.

As the house began to transform under his and Mary's hands, John decided it was time to address the exterior. The faded and peeling paint did little to dispel the ominous atmosphere that seemed to linger around the property. After a quick search on his phone for local services, he found there was only one company that specialized in exterior painting in the area. He dialed the number and waited, the line crackling slightly before a voice answered.

"Hello, this is Lee with Lee's Painting. How can I help you?" came the cheerful response.

"Hi Lee, my name is John Harper. I'm looking for someone to give my house a fresh coat of paint. It's an old place and needs some sprucing up," John explained, trying to sound as upbeat as possible.

"Absolutely, Mr. Harper. We can definitely help with that. Is the house near the North Toe River, by any chance? I think I know the one you're talking about," Lee replied, his tone knowledgeable and friendly.

"Yes, that's the one," John confirmed, a bit surprised that his new home was already known to the locals.

"Great, I can swing by tomorrow to take a look and give you a quote. What time works for you?" Lee asked.

"Morning would be perfect. Say, around ten?" John suggested, eager to keep the momentum of the renovations going.

"Ten it is. I'll see you then, Mr. Harper. We'll get that house looking like new in no time," Lee assured him, and after a few more pleasantries, they ended the call.

John set the phone down with a sigh, hoping that by maintaining a semblance of normalcy, the unsettling whispers and eerie atmosphere of the past might finally begin to fade. Yet, as he looked out the window at the encroaching twilight, a faint whistling carried on the breeze, unsettling the peace.

Mary glanced at him; eyes wide with concern. "John, you heard that right?"

"Mary, let's not do this," John replied, trying to keep his tone even. "You're probably just hearing things—it's nothing."

"How long are you going to keep dismissing this?" Mary's voice cracked slightly with frustration. "It's not just in my head, dammit. I wish you would just listen to me."

"I am listening," John countered, though his voice revealed his doubts. "I just think it's stress or the wind. These old houses make sounds."

Mary shook her head, a wry smile crossing her lips as she tried to mask her frustration. "Sure, keep telling yourself that if it helps. But even you can't ignore it forever, you know."

With a light, sarcastic chuckle, she added, "Really, John, sometimes you're such an asshole," before turning to walk away, leaving him to ponder her words as the last light of day faded from the sky.

In the afternoon, Mary stepped outside to check on the children. She found them playing near the edge of the forest, their laughter mingling with the soft rustle of the wind as it moved through the trees. Seeing them so close to the dark, enveloping woods sent a chill through her.

"Emma, Ben, come away from there!" she called, her voice trembling.

The children turned and walked back towards her; their faces flushed with excitement. "We were just exploring, Mom," Emma said, a hint of frustration in her voice. "You can let Dad know that I'm not watching YouTube." She sneered back at her mom.

"I know, but I want you to stay closer to the house," Mary replied, trying to keep her tone calm. "It's safer."

As the sun began to set across the property, the family gathered inside for dinner. The atmosphere was tense, the air thick with unspoken fears. Mary glanced out the window, the darkening forest looming ominously in the distance.

After dinner, they settled in for another quiet night. Mary tried to push aside her worries, focusing on the warmth of her family and the comfort of their new home. But as the shadows lengthened and the house grew silent, the sense of unease returned, stronger than ever.

In the distance, an owl hooted again, its call echoing through the night. Mary listened intently, waiting for any other sounds to break the silence, but none came. Was this the owl's last warning, Mary thought to herself. Maybe she should have listened the first time. Maybe she should have put her foot down and told her family that they needed to get out of there before it was too late. It wouldn't have mattered though. John was hard-headed and would never listen to Mary's growing worries.

As she lay in bed, staring at the ceiling, Mary once again found herself thinking of Barbara's warning. The folklore seemed to seep into her every thought, whispering of the impending darkness that would suffocate them all. She closed her eyes and took a deep breath, trying to convince herself it was all in her head.

The next morning, Mary woke up groggy and irritable, the remnants of the night's thoughts clinging to her like cobwebs. She went through the motions of making breakfast, her movements sluggish and automatic. John noticed her state and gave her a concerned look, but he didn't say anything, knowing she wouldn't appreciate his probing.

Emma could tell something was wrong with her mom. While her dad was away, she was the one who would comfort her when she was at her wit's end. It was hard raising two children by herself while worrying if her husband would make it home alive. The two of them spent countless hours curled up on the bed crying, but Emma was always the strong one. Ben, was still too young to know what was going on and was fortunate enough to have his mom and big sister to look after him.

Ben chattered excitedly about his big plans for the day. Emma wanted to stay inside so she could catch up with friends, while Ben was eager to check out the old barn, they had discovered the previous afternoon.

"Just stay close to the house," Mary instructed, her voice sharp. "And don't go into the forest without one of us."

Ben nodded. "We know, Mom. You told us this already."

As Emma headed upstairs and Ben out the front door, Mary and John turned their attention to the never-ending list of chores that came with moving into an old house. John continued his work in the basement, determined to make the space usable, while Mary tackled the cluttered storage closet, sorting through years of accumulated junk left behind by previous occupants.

The hours passed, and the house remained eerily quiet. Mary found herself glancing out the closet window frequently, her eyes drawn to the shadowy line of trees at the edge of their property. She still couldn't shake the feeling that something was lurking just beyond her sight, waiting.

In the basement, John worked diligently, trying to ignore the unsettling atmosphere. As he cleared out a corner piled high with old crates, he heard—a faint, almost imperceptible whistling. He paused, his heart pounding, straining to listen. The sound was so faint that he almost convinced himself he had imagined it, but then it came again, a low, haunting melody.

Lee arrived promptly at 10 a.m., pulling up in a truck emblazoned with the cheerful logo of Lee's Painting. John greeted him at the front, ready to discuss the work needed.

Mary, spotting Lee's truck from the window, called Ben inside, not wanting him to get underfoot while the adults talked business. Ben came back inside to play with a few of his toy cars and Mary felt as though she could let her guard down. He led Lee around the exterior of the house, pointing out the peeling paint and weather-beaten siding.

"It's definitely seen better days," Lee remarked, jotting notes in his notebook. "We can start with a power wash and scrape off all this old paint and caulk all the windows.

Then a primer and a couple of coats should do it. Unless we run into a bunch of dry rot, it should be a quick job."

John nodded, glad for the straightforward professional assessment. As they walked, he decided to broach the subject of the local folklore that had been weighing on his mind. "Barbara from the general store filled us in on some interesting local tales—about the woods, whistling at night, and spirits."

Lee paused, his expression turning serious. "Ah, you heard about that, huh? Barbara wasn't pulling your leg. A lot of us here really believe in those tales. Did she mention leaving out food and water at night as an offering?"

John chuckled, shaking his head. "No, she left that part out. Sounds like a waste of food and time to me."

Lee's demeanor shifted subtly, a hint of genuine concern creeping into his voice. "It's actually taken pretty seriously around here. It's not just superstition to some; it's a way of keeping peace with whatever's out there."

Attempting to keep the mood light, John joked, "Well, my boy whistled into the dark the other night and so far, nothing has happened."

The color drained from Lee's face, his eyes widening with alarm. He stopped walking, closed his notebook abruptly, and took a step back. "You shouldn't joke about that, Mr. Harper. If that's true, it's not good at all."

His laughter faded as he watched Lee's reaction transform from professional to profoundly disturbed. "You're serious? You think something's going to happen?"

Lee looked around nervously, lowering his voice. "I'm not going to stick around to find out. I'm sorry, but you might want to find someone else for this paint job. And seriously, consider what I said about the offerings... and maybe even about moving. It might already be too late."

With that, Lee headed briskly back to his truck, not once looking back. John stood there, a cold gust of wind brushing past him, carrying with it a strange whisper that sounded too much like a sigh. "Goddamn wind," he muttered to himself, a shiver running down his spine. He knew he should dismiss it as superstition, yet the fear in Lee's eyes was unsettling.

He knew he should tell Mary about this, but he hesitated, not wanting to add to her existing worries. She was already on edge, and confirming that their concerns might be valid was the last thing he wanted to do. He hoped it was all just a coincidence, but deep down, the seeds of doubt were beginning to sprout.

The Diary

As the afternoon wore on, she joined John in the basement and stumbled upon an old trunk buried under a pile of dusty blankets. Curiosity piqued, she opened it, revealing an assortment of personal items—a faded diary, yellowed letters, and a few pieces of jewelry. She carefully lifted the diary, its cover worn and cracked, and opened it to the first page.

The neat, looping handwriting belonged to a woman named Eliza. Mary began to read, her heart sinking as she absorbed the entries. Eliza had lived in the house about fifteen years ago, and her diary detailed a series of increasingly disturbing events—strange noises, whispered voices, and a growing sense of dread that had gripped her, her sister, and her mother.

Mary shivered, feeling a kinship with the long-gone woman. She knew she should share this with her husband, but the thought of worrying him even more made her hesitate. She closed the diary and tucked it back into the chest, deciding to confront him about it later.

That evening, the family gathered for dinner. The children, unaware of the tension simmering beneath the surface, chattered about their day's adventures. Emma caught up with all the teenage drama back in the city, and Ben had discovered a small pond teeming with frogs.

After dinner, as the family settled in for a movie night, the quiet of the house gave way to an unsettling atmosphere. Mary and John lounged on the couch, trying to lose themselves in the flickering images on the screen, but the silence of the house seemed almost oppressive. Then, amidst the movie's dialogue, a faint, unmistakable whistle drifted through the living room.

Mary's eyes shot towards John, her expression tight with concern. "You heard that, right?" she whispered, her voice barely above a breath to keep the children from overhearing.

He nodded subtly, a calm facade masking his alertness. "Yeah, I heard it," he whispered back, his tone reassuring. "It's just the wind. These old houses make all sorts of sounds."

Mary stood up; her movements quick but controlled. "It's coming from the basement," she murmured, her gaze fixed on the floorboards below.

Taking a deep breath, trying to instill a sense of normalcy, John suggested, "Let's check it out together. I think it's a good chance to prove it's nothing serious. Just the house settling or the wind."

Mary nodded; her hands clasped tightly together. "Okay, but let's be quiet about it."

Before heading towards the basement, He turned to Ben and Emma, who were engrossed in their movie. "Hey, kids, your mom and I need to check on something downstairs. A little project we're thinking about starting tomorrow. Just enjoy the show, and we'll be right back, okay?"

The children nodded, barely glancing away from the screen, their attention still captured by the movie.

With a quick exchange of determined glances, John and Mary crept toward the basement door, their voices barely a whisper. As they descended the creaky stairs, each step issued a protesting groan, the sounds reverberating in the chilly air of the basement. The faint whistling grew sharper, its eerie strains seeming to merge with the cold drafts that swept through the aged foundation.

The whistling intensified, morphing into an unsettling chorus that seemed to come from everywhere yet nowhere specific. As they reached the basement floor, the sound abruptly ceased, plunging the space into a heavy, enveloping silence that seemed to press against their ears.

John scanned the room with his flashlight, his heart racing. "There's nothing here," he said, his voice stern but trembling.

Mary shook her head, her eyes wide with fear. "We both heard it, dammit. Something's down here."

John had always been a skeptic when it came to the paranormal, but now, an uneasy chill was beginning to seep into his bones. Trying to rationalize the sounds, he said, "It's just the wind. This house is old, it's full of cracks and crevices. Sounds can travel in strange ways."

As they turned to leave, Mary noticed something on the floor in front of them. It was the diary she had tucked away in the chest earlier. Her breath caught in her throat, and she pointed at it, her hand shaking. "I left that diary in the basement chest."

John stared at Mary. "You probably just forgot where you put it. Things don't just move on their own. I know you believe in all that ghost shit, but it's not real."

"I swear I put it in the chest. I just know I did."

His voice carried a mixture of dismissal and an underlying tremor of doubt. "Sweetheart, you're making too much out of nothing. You're going to work yourself up over nothing if you keep this up."

Mary shot him a knowing look, her frustration mounting. "I can see it on your face. You hear it too. Don't pretend like it's not getting to you."

"It's not the noises that are worrying me, it's your obsession with them," John retorted, his voice rising slightly in his frustration. He was scared, yes, but admitting it felt like a defeat he wasn't ready to accept.

Mary shook her head, exasperated. "Talking to you is like talking to a brick wall! You're in denial, and it's driving me insane. If you can't stand by me on this, then maybe we should just drop it and go back upstairs."

Their conversation hung heavily in the air, a testament to the tension that was slowly building between them as the unexplained phenomena continued to haunt their home.

They hurried back upstairs, Mary, gripping the diary tightly in her hand. Once in the safety of the living room, Mary cautiously opened the book to a random page. Taking a deep breath to steady her nerves, she began to read in a low, trembling voice, careful to keep her words quiet enough so the children, playing at a distance, wouldn't hear the secrets it might hold.

June 12th. The whistling started again last night, coming from the basement. It's been months, and it won't stop. At first, we tried to ignore it, but it kept getting louder as if trying to lure us down there.

Mary flipped to another page, the entries becoming more frantic.

August 5th. The children are petrified. The whistling surrounds us, a relentless, maddening melody that fills every corner of the house. I've finally recognized the tune—it's "Marble Halls." I can't fathom why it haunts us so persistently. We attempted to leave, to escape the endless sound, but something mysterious holds us back. We are confined within these walls, captives to the unseen forces that torment us relentlessly.

His hand tightened on Mary's shoulder as she continued reading.

October 13th. Last night, the whistling was deafening. It felt like it was inside our heads, compelling us to answer. I fear for our sanity, for our lives. We cannot endure this much longer.

Mary threw the diary down, her heart racing. "Babe, this is... this is insane."

John began laughing hysterically. "Haha. I guess the last people who lived here had a sense of humor."

The tension in the living room escalated sharply as John and Mary continued their heated discussion, despite the presence of the kids, who were still absorbed in the tail end of their movie. Mary's hands trembled as she reached down, and picked up the diary, her voice rising with each word. "You don't think this is real? This is someone's journal. Someone's private fears and secrets."

He tried to maintain calm but his frustration was evident. "It's about as real as your grip on reality right now, crazy lady."

Fury flashed across her face as she retorted, her voice laced with bitterness, "Oh, fuck you, John. I don't give a shit if you believe me or not."

John, shocked by Mary's harsh words and escalating anger, realized this wasn't just a simple argument—it was spiraling out of control in front of Ben and Emma. He knew they needed to address this head-on, but away from the children's ears.

"Okay kiddos, it's time for bed," he said firmly, his voice cutting through the tension as he motioned for the children to head upstairs.

Ben, sensing the tension but confused, gave his dad a disappointed look. "But Dad, we haven't even finished the movie. Please can we stay up?"

"We'll finish it in the morning. Now, do as I say and get up to bed," John insisted, his tone brooking no argument.

As the children reluctantly made their way upstairs, the atmosphere between John and Mary remained charged. Once he heard the kids' bedroom doors close, John turned back to Mary, his expression a mix of concern and resolve.

"Honey, we need to talk, seriously," John began, his voice low and earnest. "This isn't like you. You're not just angry; you're terrified. What's going on? You're scaring me—and the kids."

Mary's anger momentarily gave way to a flicker of fear, her breaths short and uneven. "I'm so scared! Can't you see that? Something's wrong with this house, with this place! And that journal—it's not just stories. I feel it. And you—you just dismiss it all!"

John struggled to balance his skepticism with the fear emanating from Mary. He took a cautious step towards her, trying to bridge the gap not just physically but emotionally. "Let's figure this out together, okay? But let's keep it together, for the kids' sake."

John, recognizing the need to de-escalate the situation, and softened his tone. "Look, I won't poke fun at your fears anymore. I see they're real to you, and I should respect that," he said, reaching out in an attempt to reassure her.

However, Mary's anger was far from quelled. Feeling dismissed and patronized, she pulled away from his touch, her voice rising sharply. "Stop? Just like that? Do you think I can just stop feeling this way? You think this is easy for me?"

John took a deep breath, trying to maintain his composure as he navigated Mary's intensifying emotions. "Sweetheart, I'm trying to understand, but you have to help me here. We can't let this tear us apart."

"You're not trying to understand anything!" Mary snapped back, her frustration boiling over. "You just want everything to be simple, to make sense like in your student's damn homework problems! But it's not simple! I'm telling you something is wrong with this place, and you—you just want to pretend everything is fine!"

John, struggling to find the right words, hesitated, which only fueled Mary's fury. "Oh, fuck you, prick! You don't get it, and you never will!" Her voice echoed through the now-silent house, a stark contrast to the muted sounds of the night outside.

Seeing the frustration and hurt flicker across Mary's face, John knew he needed to tread carefully. His earlier attempts to dismiss the strange occurrences had only fueled their tension. He took a deep breath, trying to find the right words.

"Babe, listen," he began, his tone more conceding than before. "I hear the whistling too, and yeah, something feels off. But we can't let this get the best of us. If we start spiraling over this, it's only going to make things worse."

He paused, looking earnestly into her eyes. "I'm sorry for brushing it off earlier. I don't want to fight about this, especially not in front of the kids." He reached out, gently placing his hand on her shoulder in a gesture of reconciliation. "Let's try to keep a level head, for their sake, okay?"

It was a significant admission for John, one that acknowledged the severity of their situation without fully diving into the realm of the paranormal—a middle ground that he hoped would bridge the growing gap between them.

Mary, breathing heavily, her chest heaving with each breath, seemed momentarily lost in her tumult of emotions. The room fell silent, save for the faint creaking of the house—a reminder of the omnipresent atmosphere that had sparked this conflict.

John watched her warily, uncertain if his words had made any impact or if the chasm between them had grown too wide to bridge with a simple conversation. The unease of the house seemed to seep into their very interaction, coloring it with doubt and fear.

After her heated argument with John, Mary, her emotions still churning, stormed upstairs. Her hurried steps echoed through the house. As she reached the second-floor landing, a faint, sinister whistling wound its way up from the shadowed corners of the old home. It was a haunting, melodic taunt that seemed to crawl through the still air, a chilling harbinger of darker things yet to come. The melody, both alien and familiar, mocked her mounting dread, whispering promises of unseen horrors lurking just out of sight.

WHISPERS IN THE NIGHT

T he whistling from the depths of the house grew
louder as Mary stood by the children's rooms, her
nerves frayed and her heart pounding. As she looked down
the old weathered staircase, a new sound reached her ears:
a soft, rhythmic whistling coming from Ben's room.

Mary pushed the door open slowly, her heart in her
throat. There was Ben, lying on his back, eyes closed,
whistling in his sleep. The melody was eerily similar to the
one she'd heard in the basement. The sound made Mary
visibly start to shake. She needed John to see this. Maybe
then he'd believe her.

"He's... he's whistling," Mary yelled, her voice trembling.

John turned to look up towards Mary, a look of anger carved on his face. "Dammit Mary, what the hell is going on?"

John started up the staircase, but before he made it to the top, a strong breeze blew through the open windows, whipping the curtains and sending a chill through the room. The once silent night outside suddenly erupted with noise. First, the harsh cawing of crows echoed through the air, followed by the haunting hoots of owls. Moments later, the spine-chilling howls of wolves joined the cacophony. It was as if the entire forest had come alive, surrounding their house with an orchestra of dread.

"We need to get out of here," Mary said, her voice barely above a whisper, panic rising in her chest. "The animals... they are trying to warn us. They have been for the last few days but I was too afraid to tell you about it."

John nodded, his jaw set. "That's it! We'll pack in the morning. We can't stay here. You're losing your shit."

They closed Ben's door gently and retreated to their room, the night sounds were a constant reminder of the wicked presence surrounding them. Sleep was impossible, and they lay in bed, wide-eyed and tense, listening to the strange symphony outside. The whistling continued from the basement, mingling with the sounds of the night, creating an atmosphere of pure terror. John could hear it but didn't pay much attention. He was more worried about Mary and how hard she was taking all of this. She was slowly losing her mind and there was nothing he could do to convince her that it was all in their heads.

As dawn broke, the eerie sounds outside faded away, leaving an unsettling silence in their wake. John and Mary wasted no time, waking the children and instructing them to pack their belongings. Emma and Ben, sensing the urgency and fear in their parents' voices, complied without question. John had no plans of leaving the place for good but thought maybe a couple of days at a hotel might get her to calm down a bit. So, he went along with Mary's charade in hopes of not creating any more tension than there already was.

Mary hurried through the house, swiftly gathering essentials and packing them into bags. Her actions were frenzied, driven by a deep, unsettling urge to escape. Downstairs, John was loading the car, his actions precise and efficient, mirroring his wife's urgency yet trying to inject a sense of calm into the chaotic atmosphere.

The house felt increasingly claustrophobic, a tangible tension filling the air as if the space around them was compressing, squeezing tighter with every ticking second.

"We need to hurry," Mary called out from the doorway, her voice strained with anxiety.

"I know, I'm almost done here," John responded, closing the trunk with a definitive thud. "Just double-checking everything so we don't have to come back."

As he joined her at the door, he reached out, placing a reassuring hand on her shoulder. "We'll be out of here soon. Let's just keep moving, okay?"

Mary nodded, taking a deep breath, trying to find solace in John's steady presence as they prepared to leave the oppressive embrace of the house behind.

As John packed the last bag into the trunk, he noticed something strange. The whistling that they had heard all night was now eerily absent. The sudden silence was almost worse, a heavy, expectant quiet that hung in the air like a shroud.

Mary ushered the kids into the car, her eyes darting around nervously. "Let's go, John. We need to leave now."

Just as John started the car, a deep, guttural growl rumbled from the edge of the forest. Mary turned to see what looked like two girls staring at her from the darkness between the trees. Panic surged through her.

"John, Drive!" Mary yelled at the top of her lungs

John shifted the old Ford into drive, but before they could drive away, Ben suddenly jolted upright from his seat. Without warning, he flung open the car door and bolted towards the forest. John put the car back in park and tried to see where Ben was running.

"Ben!" Mary screamed, reaching out in vain. "Stop!"

John lunged towards the back seat to grab him, but Ben was too quick, darting toward the forest with unsettling determination. At the tree line, two ghostly figures awaited him: girls in tattered dresses that draped over their thin frames like spectral shrouds, one clutching a Raggedy Ann doll. Their expressions were hauntingly vacant, their hollow eyes exerting a mysterious pull on Ben.

As Ben neared the edge of the woods, the shadows swallowed him whole, and he disappeared into the darkness. All that remained was the eerie echo of his footsteps, fading into the chilling silence of the night.

John and Mary leaped from the car, their hearts pounding with fear. "Ben!" John yelled, his voice breaking. "Ben, come back!"

Mary ran towards the forest, tears streaming down her face. "Please, Ben, come back to us!"

But there was no response, only the echo of their desperate cries. The repressive silence of the forest seemed to haunt their every step, the malevolent presence watching, waiting. It was mid-morning and the sun was bright but inside the dense forest, the sun didn't have a chance to penetrate the thick canopy.

John grabbed Mary's arm, pulling her back from the edge of the forest. "We can't go in there. It's too dangerous. Let me go grab a flashlight."

Mary whirled around, her face contorted with rage and despair. "This was your stupid fucking idea! Moving out here to this godforsaken place! Now our son is gone!"

John's grip tightened, his fear and guilt boiling over. "You think I wanted this to happen? Do you think I knew this shit would happen Mary? We need to stay calm and think this through! He probably just doesn't want to leave. Ben liked it here."

John wanted to tell Mary that she was scaring the kids and that it was all her fault, but he knew that this was neither the time nor the place.

Mary struggled against him, trying to break free. "Calm? Our son is out there. God knows where, and you want me to stay calm? Didn't you see those people out there? They took him."

John held her close, her warm tears running down John's neck. "We'll find him. I promise. But we can't just run in there blind. We need to get help."

Mary collapsed against him, her sobs wracking her body. "What have we done, babe? What have we done?"

The forest stood dark and foreboding before them, the eerie whistling from the night before still haunting their thoughts. Finding Ben was now their urgent priority, but both Mary and John felt a chilling anticipation that the worst was yet to come.

The silence of the forest felt suffocating, almost tangible, as if the air itself was thickening around them. The muted morning light struggled to pierce the dense canopy, casting ghostly shadows that twisted and flickered across the forest floor. Every rustle and whisper of the woods seemed loaded with intent, the ancient trees standing as silent sentinels to their deep, dark secrets.

"What if we can't find him?" Mary's voice broke the oppressive quiet, her tone laced with fear.

"We will," John replied firmly, trying to muster confidence he barely felt. "I'll find Ben, don't worry. Just stay close and keep calling for him."

John pushed forward, leading the way deeper into the woods. Every step felt heavier, the unknown of the forest weighing on him, but his resolve to find his son drove him onward, cutting through the thick air and the lingering dread of what might lie ahead.

"Go back and get Emma, then go inside and call the police," John said, his voice urgent but controlled. "I'll stay out here and look for Ben. The sun is starting to shed some light in the forest so maybe I can track where he went."

Mary hesitated, her eyes wide with fear and desperation, but she nodded and ran out of the woods and back to the house, her footsteps crunching on the gravel driveway. John turned to head deeper into the forest, his heart pounding, his throat dry.

"Ben!" he called, his voice cracking with a mix of fear and hope. "Ben, where are you?"

His words seemed to vanish into the depths of the forest, swallowed by the dense undergrowth and the towering trees. The only response was the rustling of leaves and the distant, mournful cries of the crows.

John took a step closer as he inched closer to a clearing, his eyes scanning the dark shadows between the trees. "Ben! Please, answer me!"

The silence that followed was deafening. John felt a cold sweat break out on his forehead, his hands trembling. He could feel the spiteful presence of the forest watching him, taunting him. He continued walking and found himself back near the driveway.

There is no way I just walked in a goddamn circle! How the hell did I end up back here?

Behind him, the screen door creaked as Mary stepped back outside. John turned to see her walking slowly towards him, her face pale and stricken. She had the phone clutched in her hand; her eyes filled with tears.

"What did they say?" John asked, dread pooling in his stomach.

Mary swallowed hard, her voice barely a whisper. "The sheriff said he'll be out here soon, but... but he said Ben isn't the first kid to go missing out here. He said the chances of finding him are slim to none."

John's heart sank, a cold, hollow feeling spreading through his chest. "No, we can't give up. We have to find him. We have to."

Mary's shoulders slumped; her defeat palpable. "What are we going to do? How are we going to find him?"

John clenched his fists, his resolve hardening. "We can't just stand here. We have to start looking. We'll search the forest ourselves."

He took Mary's hand, leading her towards the dark tree line. The forest loomed before them, an impenetrable wall of shadows and whispers. They stepped into the undergrowth, the air growing colder, the light dimming as the trees closed in around them.

"Ben!" John called again, his voice echoing through the trees. "Ben, please answer us!"

The forest seemed to mock them, the rustling leaves and distant animal cries creating an eerie symphony. Mary shivered, her grip on John's hand tightening.

"Do you feel that?" she whispered; her breath visible in the cold air. "It's so... cold."

John nodded, his breath fogging in the chill. "I know. We have to keep moving. He can't be far."

They pushed deeper into the forest, their footsteps muffled by the thick carpet of leaves and moss. The trees seemed to close in around them, their twisted branches reaching out like the forest was pulling them in. Pulling them closer to their impending doom. Shadows danced at the edges of their vision, and the faint, haunting whistling seemed to follow them, growing louder and more insistent.

"Ben!" Mary cried, her voice breaking. "Please, come back to us!"

A sudden movement caught John's eye, a flash of something pale darting between the trees. "There!" he shouted, pointing. "I saw something!"

They hurried towards the spot, their hearts pounding, hope flaring briefly. But when they reached it, there was nothing but the thick, impenetrable darkness of the forest.

Mary fell to her knees, her sobs wracking her body. "He's gone. He's really fucking gone."

John knelt beside her, wrapping his arms around her. "We can't give up. We can't. We'll find him, sweetheart. I promise."

The forest continued to close in around them, the dark presence pressing down on them, pulling its way into their lungs and sinking its dark fangs into their every thought. The whistling grew louder, more insistent, a sinister melody that wrapped around their minds, fraying their sanity.

As they sat there, enveloped by the darkness, Emma's voice broke the silence. "Mom? Dad?" she called out, her tone eerily calm.

John and Mary turned to see Emma standing at the edge of the forest, her eyes wide and unfocused. "Sweetheart, go back to the house," John said, trying to keep his voice steady. "It's not safe out here."

Emma didn't move. Instead, she tilted her head to the side, as if listening to something only she could hear. "Can you hear it?" she whispered. "The whistling... it's calling to me."

Mary's heart clenched with fear. "Emma, please, go back to the house."

But Emma took a step forward, her eyes fixed on the dark depths of the forest. "It's beautiful," she murmured. "I want to see where it leads."

John rushed to her, grabbing her by the shoulders and shaking her gently. "Emma, snap out of it! We need to find your brother!"

Emma blinked, her eyes focusing on John. "Dad... I... I saw him. In the forest. He was... different."

John felt a cold dread settle over him. "What do you mean, different?"

Emma's eyes glazed over again. "He looked... happy. Like he belonged there."

Mary clutched John's arm, her voice trembling. "Something is happening to her. We need to get her back to the house."

John tightened his grip on Emma's shoulder, his decision set. "Mary, take her back to the house. I'm going to keep looking for Ben."

Reluctantly, Mary nodded, her face pale with worry. She took Emma's hand, squeezing it reassuringly as they turned to head back to the house. The haunting whistle seemed to follow them, echoing louder with each step as if mocking their retreat.

Once inside the house, the walls felt like a thin barrier against the encroaching darkness outside. Mary, trembling, her hands, picked up the phone again in a desperate attempt to call and see if the Sheriff was on his way, but found the line disturbingly dead. She then ran outside looking for John. "Shit, the phone... it's not working," she yelled out in John's direction, her voice echoing slightly.

Back in the forest, John's face set into a grim expression as he processed the news. "We're on our own then," he muttered to himself, steeling his nerves.

Meanwhile, Mary and Emma waited in the safety of the house, the atmosphere weighing heavily upon them. Emma sat by the window, her eyes distant and haunted as if she could still hear the whispers of the forest. Mary stayed close, watching over her daughter with a protective vigilance, her mind racing with worry for her children and her husband who was still searching in the dark.

After hours of searching through the dense, whispering forest with no sign of Ben, John finally returned to the house, his clothes damp with sweat and his expression etched with fatigue and frustration. The door creaked loudly as he stepped inside, the sound cutting through the tense silence that had enveloped the home.

Mary, who had been pacing near the window, turned sharply at the sound of the door. Her face, drawn with worry, brightened momentarily with hope, but it faded quickly when she saw John's solitary figure and the grim set of his jaw. "John, any sign of him?" her voice trembled with barely contained fear.

John shook his head, a mix of anger and disbelief coloring his tone. "No, nothing. It's like he was... it was as if he was running away from me. I kept seeing flashes of someone darting between the trees, just glimpses at the edge of my vision. But every time I got to where I thought I saw him, there was nobody there."

Mary's hands flew to her mouth, her eyes widening with terror. "What do you mean? Like someone was leading you on, or..." her voice trailed off, unable to finish the thought.

"It felt like that," John admitted, his voice heavy. "Or like something was playing tricks on me. I don't know, but it wasn't normal. I called out, ran after what I saw, and checked every possible hiding spot I could find. Nothing. It's like he just vanished."

The couple stood in the living room, the weight of John's words thick in the air. Mary felt a cold dread creep over her, the eerie events aligning disturbingly with the local legends they had been told.

"We need to call the authorities, John. We need help," Mary insisted, her voice firm despite her visible shaking.

John nodded, his decision firm despite the earlier failed attempt to use the phone. "I'll try the phone again, see if the line's back up. If not, I'll drive into town. We need to report him missing, get a search team out here."

The afternoon stretched on, fraught with tension and unspoken fears, as they waited for dawn, hoping for a miracle that would bring Ben back to them safely.

John kept going back into the forest every few hours trying to track Ben's location but he found nothing. The sheriff never arrived and as night fell, the whistling returned, louder and more insistent. The house felt like it was closing in on them, the walls creaking and groaning. Shadows danced in the corners, and the air grew colder.

John and Mary huddled together; their fear palpable. Emma stood by the window; her face illuminated by the pale moonlight. "It's time," she said softly, turning to face them. "We have to go back to the forest. I know where Ben is."

John shook his head, his voice desperate. "Emma, I've been out there all day. I can't find him."

But Emma's eyes were vacant, her expression serene. "We don't have a choice. The forest is calling us. We have to answer."

As the whistling grew louder, John and Mary knew they were trapped, caught in a nightmare they couldn't escape.

THE RETURN

The oppressive whistling that had filled the house suddenly ceased, plunging everything into a suffocating silence once again. The forest outside seemed to hold its breath, the eerie quiet settling over the family like a shroud. John and Mary exchanged a fearful glance, their hearts pounding in the stillness.

The shadows in the room seemed to grow darker, more ominous, as the silence stretched on. Mary clutched John's arm; her eyes wide with terror. Emma stood by the window; her vacant gaze fixed on the moonlit forest.

And then, breaking the silence like a sudden crash of thunder, the front door flung open. Ben stood there, looking annoyed and impatient. "I thought we were leaving. I've been waiting in the car forever."

John and Mary stared at him, disbelief and relief flooding their senses. Mary was the first to move, rushing to Ben and pulling him into a tight embrace. "Ben! Oh my God, you're okay!"

Ben looked confused, trying to wriggle free from Mary's grasp. "Yeah, I'm fine. Why wouldn't I be?"

John joined them, his voice shaky. "Ben, you... you ran into the forest. We've been looking for you all day."

Ben frowned, shaking his head. "No, I didn't. I've been in the car the whole time. What's going on?"

Emma turned from the window, her eyes blinking and struggling to focus on her brother as if she were snapping out of a trance. "Ben, are you sure? We saw you run into the woods."

Ben's frown deepened. "I'm sure. I was waiting in the car. I got bored, so I came back to see what was taking so long."

Mary's relief began to mingle with confusion and fear. "What the hell's happening? How is this possible?"

John shook his head, his mind racing. "I don't know. I wish I had an answer, but I can't explain what's going on."

John peered out through the open door, his gaze shifting between the ominous expanse of the woods and the safety of his home. Just at the edge of the forest, two eerie figures stood—the same two girls they had seen earlier in the day, their smiles unsettlingly serene as they waved at him. With a shiver, John pulled his head back inside and quickly locked the door, sealing off the outside world. The oppressive silence of the forest hung heavily in the air, but within the walls of their house, his family remained safe—for now.

As the reality of what had just happened began to sink in, the terror they felt turned into a gnawing dread. John and Mary sat on the living room couch, their faces pale and drawn. Emma hovered near the window; her gaze distant. Ben, seemingly oblivious to the fear that gripped his family, played with his toy cars on the floor.

"John, we can't ignore this," Mary said, her voice trembling. "Something is happening. Maybe that cashier was right. It's either that or we're losing our minds."

John rubbed his temples, trying to think clearly. "I know. Shit... I know. But what can we do? We'll leave first thing in the morning. Ben is safe now, but I'm worried. What if this... thing follows us?"

Mary's eyes filled with tears. "What if it's already inside us, babe? What if this thing wants us to go crazy?"

Emma turned away from the window, her eyes seeming to stare right through her parents. "I see things," she whispered. "In the shadows. Faces. They watch me... they watch all of us."

John and Mary exchanged a terrified glance. "What kind of faces, Emma?" John asked, trying to keep his voice steady.

"Old faces. Angry faces. They want something from us," Emma said, her voice distant and hollow. "One of them told me that we were meant to be here. That we were part of the family."

John stood up, his hands shaking. "Fuck this. We need to get out of here right now!"

As he reached for the phone, the lights flickered and went out, plunging the house into darkness. The oppressive silence returned, heavier than before. The only light came from the dim glow of the moon filtering through the windows.

Mary clung to John, her breath coming in ragged gasps. "What's happening?"

Before he could answer, the whistling started again, louder and more insistent. It seemed to come from all around them, wrapping around their minds, pressing in on every fiber of their beings. The walls of the house creaked and groaned, as if under some immense pressure.

Ben's eyes glazed over, and he began to whistle along with the eerie melody, his small body swaying to the rhythm. Mary grabbed him, shaking him. "Ben! Stop it! Please!"

But Ben continued, his eyes unfocused, lost in some dark trance. The whistling grew louder, more frenzied, filling the room with its unnerving tune.

John grabbed a flashlight from the drawer and turned it on, the beam cutting through the darkness. "We need to get to the car. Now!"

They moved towards the door, but as they did, the shadows seemed to come alive, writhing and twisting, forming grotesque shapes that reached out towards them. Faces emerged from the darkness, twisted and enraged, their eyes glowing with evil light.

"Run!" John shouted, pushing Mary, Emma, and Ben towards the door.

They stumbled outside, the whistling following them, growing louder and more desperate. The cold night air hit them like a ton of bricks, and they raced towards the car, John holding Ben tightly.

As they reached the car, the engine roared to life, but the whistling didn't stop. It grew louder, more persistent, a cacophony of madness that threatened to tear their minds apart.

"Go!" Mary screamed; her eyes wide with terror. "Get us out of here!"

John's grip on the steering wheel tightened, his knuckles white. "Hold on!"

But as he shifted into gear, the car lurched violently, throwing them against their seats. The engine sputtered and died.

Mary's breath came in short, panicked gasps. "What do we do?"

John's mind raced, desperation clawing at him as he tried to get the car to turn over but to no avail. "We have to get back inside. Maybe if we just ignore whatever the hell this is, it will go away."

They stumbled back into the house, the whistling following them like a dark specter. Inside, the shadows seemed to pulse with spiteful energy, the unrecognizable faces watching them.

Emma's voice was barely a whisper. "They're here. They're inside."

John grabbed a knife from the kitchen, his hands shaking. "Stay together."

As they huddled in the living room, the whistling reached a fever pitch, the walls shaking with the intensity of the sound. The faces in the shadows grew clearer, their expressions twisted with both rage and sorrow.

Suddenly, Ben's body went rigid, and he let out a bloodcurdling scream. His eyes rolled back, and he convulsed violently, the whistling pouring from his lips in a maddening torrent.

Mary screamed, holding her son tightly. "Ben! No!"

John moved towards Ben trying to pull him away from whatever had a grasp on him. "Whatever the hell you are, let go of my son."

Emma's eyes were wide with terror. "It's too late. They're taking him."

The shadows surged forward, wrapping around Ben, and pulling him away from his mother. John slashed at them with the knife, but it passed through the darkness harmlessly.

"Let him go!" John screamed; his voice raw with desperation.

From the shadows, a voice emerged, chilling and resonant, cloaked in a sinister yet strangely paternal tone. "You are my family now," Harold, known to the townsfolk as Father, declared, his words echoing through the darkness. "There's nowhere to hide, nowhere to run."

Mary, her heart pounding with fear yet laced with curiosity, mustered the courage to respond. "What do you want with us, Harold? Why are you doing this?"

"Join us, and together we will reclaim this town," Harold continued, ignoring her questions. "The people here will learn the truth of what happened—they will feel the pain I have suffered, every single night."

Mary, trembling yet defiant, pressed further. "What pain? What truth are you talking about?"

"Don't resist, Mary. Embrace it. Embrace your destiny with us," Harold urged, his voice softening, trying to coax her into submission. His words, though meant to seduce, carried an undercurrent of sorrow, blending fear with a twisted sense of care.

"Why should I trust you?" Mary countered, her voice steady despite the fear that gripped her. "You haunt us, threaten us—how can that be for any good?"

Harold's voice grew colder, yet a note of desperation seeped through. "Because we are bound by more than you know. This town, these people... they turned their backs on me, left me to suffer alone. But you, you can help me make it right. You and your family."

Mary felt the darkness press in, the weight of Harold's presence bearing down on her. "I won't let fear rule me,

Harold. We will fight you, fight this curse you're trying to spread."

Harold chuckled, a sound that sent chills down her spine. "Very well, Mary. But remember, the night is long, and I have been waiting a very long time to share my story. You will see, in time, that we are not so different."

The conversation left Mary shaken, her resolve tested yet firmer than before. She knew now that the fight would be harder than she'd imagined, a battle not just for her family's safety, but for the soul of Micaville itself.

From the enveloping darkness, a voice emerged, chilling and ominously paternal, sending waves of terror through Mary. "You are my family now," it declared, the tone authoritative and unsettling. "There is nowhere to hide, nowhere to run."

Mary, gripped by an overwhelming fear that brought tears to her eyes, barely managed to stammer a response. "Who are you? What do you want from us?"

"Join us, and together we will reclaim this town," the voice continued, implacable and cold. "The people here will learn the truth of what happened—they will feel the pain I have suffered, every single night."

Struggling against the paralyzing terror, Mary whispered, "Why us? We're just a family. We don't belong to this... this nightmare!"

"Don't resist, Mary. Embrace it. Embrace your destiny with us," the voice coaxed, its tone softening to a deceitful gentleness. "Do you think it was mere coincidence that brought you to this house? No. You were led here, guided by forces beyond your understanding, by me and my 'family.' There is a reason you are here at this very house, at this very time."

"Why? Why us?" Mary cried, the tears streaming down her face as she clutched at the air, as if trying to grasp some shred of reality to anchor her.

"Because we are bound by more than you can yet understand," the voice replied, now a mix of sympathy and malevolence. "This town, its history, its pain, it all leads back to here—to me. And now, to you and your family."

The revelation left Mary sobbing uncontrollably, her body racked with fear. The weight of the voice's presence was oppressive, making the air around her feel thick and suffocating.

The shadows pulsed, the whistling growing louder, more frenzied. Ben's body was lifted into the air, his screams mingling with the eerie melody. The faces in the shadows watched with cruel delight, their eyes glowing with a vindictive light.

Mary reached out, her voice breaking. "Please, don't take him! Please, I beg you."

But the shadows paid no heed, pulling Ben deeper into their dark embrace. The whistling reached a crescendo, a symphony of madness that threatened to thrust them into insanity.

And then, with a final, deafening note, the whistling stopped. The shadows receded, leaving the family huddled together, their minds shattered by the horrors they had witnessed.

Ben was gone.

The silence that followed was heavy with grief and despair. John and Mary held each other, their sobs echoing in the empty house. Emma stood by the window, her eyes vacant, lost in the darkness that had claimed her brother.

The forest outside was still, the presence that had haunted them now silent. But the memory of the whistling, and the faces in the shadows, would linger forever, a reminder of the horror that had claimed their minds and their son.

Mary began breathing heavily and running through the house screaming Ben's name. John noticed her hyperventilating and tried to calm her down. "We'll find him, honey, don't you worry."

Mary's eyes frantically darted around, and she lashed out at her husband. "He's gone. He's fucking gone! Why don't you stop acting like everything is going to be alright? We just lost our son for the second time in one day and all you're doing is fucking standing there.

Her breathing became even heavier and before John had a chance to catch her, she collapsed to the floor.

The Next Morning

Morning light filtered weakly through the curtains, casting pale, thin beams into the Harper household. The oppressive atmosphere from the night before seemed to have dissipated, leaving behind an eerie calm. Mary awoke, her heart pounding, and her mind racing with the memories of the previous night. She sat up in bed, drenched in sweat, the vivid horrors still fresh in her mind.

But as she looked around, she realized something was off. John was lying next to her, fast asleep, his breathing deep and even. The sight of him sleeping so peacefully felt jarring compared to the tragedy that had transpired just hours ago.

Mary quickly got out of bed and rushed to the children's rooms. She found Emma and Ben both still in bed, sleeping soundly. Panic surged through her—how could they sleep so peacefully after what had happened? How and when did Ben come back?

"Ben! Emma!" she called, shaking them gently. "Wake up!"

Ben stirred, blinking groggily. "Mom? What's going on?"

Emma rubbed her eyes, got out of bed, walked to her doorway and looked up at their mother with confusion. "Why do you keep waking us up so early?"

Mary's heart raced. "Don't you remember? Last night... the forest, the whistling, Ben... you were taken!"

Ben frowned, sitting up. "Taken? What are you talking about, Mom? I was just in bed."

Emma looked at Mary with concern. "Mom, are you okay? You sound crazy."

Mary stumbled back, her mind reeling. "No, no, this isn't right. You were there, you both were. The shadows, the whistling... it was real!"

John appeared at the doorway; his expression tired but calm. "Mary, what's going on? Why are you waking them? They both had a long day playing, and we stayed up real late watching movies together."

"Babe, don't you remember? Last night, the whistling, the shadows... Ben was taken!" Mary's voice was urgent, filled with a terror that chilled the air.

John's brow furrowed in confusion as he looked from Mary to the children, who were clearly safe and unharmed. "Sweetheart, what are you talking about?" he asked, his voice steady but laced with concern. "Look, Ben's right here. Nothing happened last night."

Mary's eyes darted wildly between John and the children, her breaths quick and sharp with panic. "Please, you have to believe me—it was all too real," she gasped, her voice trembling with urgency. "I saw everything—Ben ran into the woods, and when he came back, something had changed. And then, those dark shadows, they just enveloped him right in front of me," she insisted, her words spilling out in a torrent of fear.

Her voice dropped to a whisper, fraught with fear, "The shadows... they spoke. They said we're part of their family now, that we were brought here for some purpose. That's what's terrifying me."

John, visibly trying to maintain a calm demeanor amidst the chaos, replied with a measured tone. "Sweets, I know something strange is going on, and I'm not dismissing what you felt or heard. But you're letting it get to you too much."

Emma, trying to cut through the tension with the straightforwardness of a typical teenager, chimed in, "Mom, could it be like stress or something? This house is super old and creepy."

John nodded at Emma's input, then continued, "Exactly, and honestly, it might be something like mold or asbestos in this old house that's messing with us, making us feel and see things that aren't there. We're all on edge. I think we should get the place tested—just to rule out any environmental causes that could be affecting our heads."

Mary, though still shaken, took a moment to consider John's words. The idea that their experiences could have a rational explanation brought her a sliver of comfort, though the fear was not entirely dispelled. "Okay, maybe you're right. Maybe getting the house tested is a good start," she conceded, her voice still laden with worry but slightly relieved at the thought of a tangible, logical step forward.

John placed a gentle hand on Mary's shoulder, his voice low and steady despite the turmoil inside him. "Let's try to stay calm for the kids," he urged, his eyes flicking toward their children, who were visibly shaken. Deep down, John grappled with the reality that what was unfolding was no mere product of mold—it was real, terrifyingly real. Yet, he clung to the notion as a lifeline to offer some semblance of normalcy, hoping to soothe Mary's rising panic.

The family's tense dynamic hung in the balance as they contemplated their next steps, the unknown still looming large but now tempered with a plan that offered a hint of control.

John stepped closer, placing a comforting hand on her shoulder, which she instinctively shrugged off. "It was just a nightmare. We are all here, nothing out of the ordinary happened. The kids are safe," he reassured her, gesturing towards Ben and Emma, who watched the scene with a mix of confusion and fright.

"But it felt so real," Mary whispered, her gaze unfocused, as if trying to discern dream from reality.

John sighed, glancing at the children who clung to each other, seeking comfort. "Let's try to calm down, for the kids," he suggested gently. "We're all safe here. It was just a bad dream, that's all."

Mary nodded slowly, the lines of fear softening as she looked at her children, reassured by their presence yet haunted by the vividness of her nightmare. The unease lingered, a silent whisper that maybe, just maybe, what she saw wasn't just a dream. But for now, she had to hold onto the reality that her family was safe, right there with her.

John exchanged a concerned look with Ben and Emma. "Why don't we all go downstairs and have some breakfast? Try not to make a big deal about this. You're freaking out the kids."

Reluctantly, Mary followed them downstairs. The house was quiet, the morning light casting a serene glow over everything. It was as if the horrors of the night before had never happened. But Mary couldn't shake the feeling that something was terribly wrong.

As they sat at the kitchen table, John and the children exchanged worried glances. Mary could see the doubt in their eyes, the worry that she was losing her mind.

"Sweetheart, we need to talk about this," John said gently. "I think you might have had a very vivid nightmare. It's not uncommon after a stressful move. God only knows the nightmares I have just about every night. You just can't let them get to you. My PTSD therapist said that if I lose too much sleep over them then it will just make things worse. Memory loss, irritability, and difficulty concentrating. Sound familiar? I just think you need some sleep."

Mary shook her head, her hands trembling. "No, John, it wasn't a nightmare. I know what I saw. Ben was taken, and there were shadows, and that damn whistling..."

Emma reached out and took her mother's hand. "Mom, we love you, but you need to rest. Maybe you're just really stressed out and like Dad said, maybe we have a mold problem. You have been in the house a lot."

Ben nodded; his eyes wide with concern. "Yeah, Mom. We're all okay. Maybe you just need to take a day to come play with us. You haven't seen all the cool stuff around the property."

Mary looked at their faces, her heart breaking. They didn't believe her. They thought she was crazy. But she knew what she had seen, what she had felt. The memories were too vivid, too real to be just a nightmare.

John put his arm around her shoulders. "We can talk to someone if you need to. A professional. I can give my old shrink a call. I know she works miracles in the VA. Maybe it would help. Or maybe just a day of getting some fresh air. I'll try to call a home inspector out here today and see if they can find anything that may be causing this."

Mary pulled away from him, standing up abruptly. "No, I don't need a doctor. I need you to believe me."

John sighed; his expression pained. "Sweetheart, we do believe you. We believe that you believe it. But right now, you need to take care of yourself. Maybe Ben is right. Why don't you take the day to play with the kiddos."

Mary felt a wave of despair wash over her. She was alone in this. The horrors she had witnessed were real, but no one believed her. She sat back down, her hands shaking.

"Please, just listen to me," she stood up and pleaded. "Last night, something terrible happened. And I don't know how or why, but it was real. I feel like we can't just ignore this."

John nodded slowly. "Okay. We'll keep an eye out. But for now, let's try to stay calm and take things one step at a time."

Mary knew they were just humoring her, but she nodded, too exhausted to argue. She sat at the table, staring at her hands, feeling the weight of their disbelief crushing her. She had to find a way to prove that she wasn't crazy, that the horrors she had seen were real.

But for now, all she could do was wait and hope that the truth would reveal itself before it was too late.

The sun rose higher in the sky, casting a golden glow over the Harper household. The oppressive weight of the previous night seemed to lift with the morning light, replaced by the soft rustle of leaves in the gentle breeze. The air was cool and crisp, the perfect morning in the countryside, yet Mary couldn't shake the unease that clung to her like a shadow.

John finished his coffee, giving Mary a reassuring smile. "It's going to be a beautiful day. Maybe some fresh air will do us all good."

Mary's grip on her mug tightened, her knuckles white. "Just... keep an eye on the kids. Please."

John nodded, his smile fading slightly. "Of course."

Emma and Ben, full of energy, dashed outside the moment breakfast was done. Their laughter rang through the yard, innocent and carefree. They raced across the grass, Emma's long blonde hair streaming behind her, Ben's feet pounding the earth with joyous abandon.

"Stay where I can see you!" Mary called after them, her voice edged with desperation. She stood in the doorway, watching them with an intensity that bordered on panic.

John placed a gentle hand on her shoulder. "They're fine, Mary. Let them play."

Mary turned to him, her eyes pleading. "Please, make sure they stay out of the woods."

John nodded, trying to calm her. "Kids, stay in the yard. No going into the woods."

Emma rolled her eyes but nodded, while Ben gave a thumbs-up before diving back into their game. Mary watched them, her heart hammering in her chest, as John led her to a chair on the porch.

A Beautiful Day

The yard was a picture of tranquility. Sunlight filtered through the trees, casting dappled shadows on the grass. A soft breeze rustled the leaves on the trees, carrying the scent of pine and earth. Birds chirped cheerfully from the branches, and somewhere in the distance, a brook babbled over stones. There was so much beauty out there, but Mary was too lost in her thoughts to take it all in.

She sat on the edge of her chair, her eyes never leaving the children. Emma and Ben played tag; their laughter infectious. They seemed so happy and normal, yet Mary's skin prickled with unease. Every shadow seemed a threat, every rustle a warning.

John settled beside her, watching the kids with a smile. "See? They're having fun. Nothing to worry about."

Mary forced a smile, her fingers digging into the armrests of the chair. "I just... can't shake this feeling, babe."

John took her hand, his touch warm and comforting. "We'll get through this, together." He then pulled out his phone and tapped quickly, looking up local home inspectors. "Ah, here we go. I'll give these guys a call and see if they can shed any light on what might be happening."

He dialed the number, and a voice with a distinct Southern drawl answered. "Hello, this is Beau with Micaville Home Inspections. How can I assist y'all today?"

John cleared his throat and began describing their situation. "Morning, Beau. My name's John Harper. We just moved into an older home out here and, well, we've been having some strange experiences—mood swings, hallucinations. I'm not sure if mold can do that, but we're hoping to rule everything out."

"Ahh, y'all must be the new folks up by the Toe River. Yep, toxic mold can sure cause a heap of problems, including hallucinations, brain fog, dizziness, not to mention anxiety and depression," Beau explained with a knowledgeable tone.

John glanced at Mary, who was listening intently to the conversation, and gave her a reassuring smile before continuing. "That makes a lot of sense. Could you come out and check our place for mold?"

"Let me peek at our schedule and I'll get back to y'all," Beau responded. "Is this the best number to reach you at?"

"Yes, please call me back anytime. The sooner, the better."

"I'll make sure to call y'all within the next few days. We're booked up for about a week, but keep that fresh air flowin' through your house in the meantime."

"Thanks, Beau. Appreciate it," John replied, a hint of relief in his voice. "Looking forward to hearing from you."

"Thank you for callin', John. Y'all have a wonderful day now," Beau said before the line went dead.

John hung up and turned back to Mary. "See, I told you there would be a logical explanation for all this."

"I sure hope you're right, babe."

As the day progressed, the sun climbed higher in the sky, casting a warm, golden glow over the yard. The sky was a brilliant blue, scattered with fluffy white clouds—an idyllic scene that would normally have soothed Mary's spirits. However, today was different. Despite the serene setting, a knot of anxiety tightened in her stomach. She remained skeptical that what she had witnessed could be attributed to mold. The experiences felt too vivid, too tangible to be simply brushed off as hallucinations induced by environmental factors. Her doubt lingered, heavy and persistent, coloring her perception of the otherwise beautiful day.

Emma and Ben chased each other around the yard, their laughter mingling with the sounds of nature. They found a patch of wildflowers near the edge of the woods and began picking bouquets, their giggles floating back to the porch.

Mary's eyes flicked nervously to the tree line, shadows lurking just beyond. "Kids, come closer to the house!" she called, her voice tinged with fear.

Emma turned, holding up a handful of flowers. "We're just picking these, Mom. We'll stay where you can see us."

Mary nodded, swallowing her panic. She could see them, but the forest seemed to loom, dark and threatening, a constant reminder of the night before.

John squeezed her hand. "They're fine, Mary. They're right there."

The hours passed slowly, the beautiful day at odds with the dread that gnawed at Mary. She watched the kids with an intensity that left her exhausted, every fiber of her being focused on keeping them safe.

John and Mary sat together on the front porch as they watched Ben and Emma play in the yard. The simple joy of their laughter provided a brief respite from the undercurrent of tension that had woven itself into their daily lives.

Trying to shift the mood, John turned to Mary with an optimistic tone. "How about we start planning that garden you've wanted? We could set up some raised beds right over there," he suggested, pointing to a sunny patch of the yard.

Mary's eyes followed his gesture, then returned to their children, a faint smile touching her lips. "That sounds lovely," she responded, her voice carrying a hint of genuine interest for the first time in days. "Maybe some tomatoes, peppers... and herbs? Could be nice."

John nodded, pleased to see a spark of her old enthusiasm. "Exactly, let's do that. It'll be a great project for us." He paused, watching Emma chase Ben around a tree. The normalcy of the scene made him hesitate to bring up anything that could cast a shadow over the moment. However, the concern lingered, unspoken, about when the painter would return to finish their house.

Mary seemed to read his mind. "And the painting? Did Lee say when he might come back to finish up?" she asked, her tone casual but her eyes searching his for an answer.

John shifted slightly, weighing his words carefully. "Well, he's pretty tied up with other jobs. Might be a bit before he can come back," he said, opting not to mention Lee's actual refusal and the unsettling reasons behind it. "I'll keep on it, though. Don't worry."

"Okay," Mary said, turning her attention back to the children. She seemed to accept his explanation, at least for now. "Let's not let it drag on too long, though."

"Of course not," John assured her, reaching over to gently squeeze her hand. They both turned their gaze back to Ben and Emma. The simple act of planning a garden together on a peaceful afternoon was a small, vital step toward reclaiming the sense of safety and home they both yearned for.

The afternoon sun danced across the yard as Ben, still flushed from playing, looked up at his parents with wide, hopeful eyes. "Can we have ice cream, Mom?"

John, catching the hint, smiled and ruffled Ben's hair. "Well, we do need to go back into town for some groceries. Let's take a trip. Maybe we can pick up something for dinner while we're out."

Mary's heart skipped a beat. The idea of leaving and then coming back filled her with unease, but she forced a smile for the kids' sake. "All right, let's go."

Mary wanted to tell John that they should go back to the city and leave this place for good, but she knew John would never go for that.

The drive into town was uneventful, the countryside bathed in the gorgeous afternoon light. The oppressive fear that had haunted them seemed to lift slightly, replaced by the normalcy of a family outing. Mary stared out the window, her mind racing with the memories of Ben being lifted and swallowed by the dark shadows. The memory of him running into the woods, and of Emma who seemed to be taken over by some evil spirit.

They arrived at the J.R. Thomas General Store, the familiar bell tinkling as they entered. The store clerk, Barbara, looked up from her magazine, her beautiful aging face crinkling in a welcoming smile. "Well, hello again. Back for more supplies?"

John nodded, leading the kids towards the ice cream freezer. "Yeah, and maybe some dinner ideas."

Mary hung back, her heart pounding. She approached the counter, her voice low and trembling. "Barbara, I need to talk to you. About last night."

Barbara's expression shifted, her smile fading. "What happened, hon?"

Mary glanced over her shoulder, making sure John and the kids were out of earshot. "There was whistling... from the forest. And... Ben... he disappeared into the woods. Then he just showed up again, like nothing happened. She wanted to tell Barbara everything but didn't want to come off too crazy.

Barbara's face paled, her eyes widening in fear. "Someone whistled back, didn't they?"

Mary's breath caught in her throat. "Yes, but... how did you know?"

Barbara leaned in, her voice low and tinged with a hint of her Southern drawl, trying to keep the mood light. "Now, honey, best you all stay put in that house come nightfall. If you hear a whistle or see somethin' odd out by them trees, just tell yourself, 'No, I didn't.' Ain't nothin' but the wind playing tricks on your mind."

Mary, a knot of worry tightening in her chest, looked at Barbara skeptically. "Are you saying it's all in our heads?"

"Oh, not exactly, darlin'," Barbara replied with a reassuring smile. "This land, well, it's got its quirks, you know? The old tales talk of spirits and shadows, but I reckon they're just stories stirred up to explain the unexplainable."

"But what if it's something more? What if it's real?" Mary pressed; her voice tinged with concern.

Barbara chuckled softly, trying to ease Mary's fear. "Now, I've lived here my whole life, and I tell you, the less mind you pay to such things, the less they bother you. These spirits, if that's what you wanna call 'em, they feed off fear and fuss. Best way to deal with 'em is to ignore 'em. Deny 'em any hold over you."

Mary nodded slowly, absorbing Barbara's advice, but her expression remained troubled.

Barbara patted Mary's hand gently. "Just keep to yourselves, keep calm, and carry on as normal. I know it sounds simple, but really, darlin', it's the best way. All this talk of haunts and spooks, it's easy to get caught up in it. But remember, it's your home now. Claim it, and don't let old ghost stories chase you out."

Their conversation meandered a bit more, with Barbara continuing to downplay the severity of the situation while subtly reinforcing the importance of staying put. Her words, intended to comfort, left Mary with a mix to mull over.

Mary nodded. "Thank you. I'll do that."

John made his way toward Mary and Barbara, his steps measured, a woven basket hooked securely in the crook of his arm. The basket was thoughtfully packed with the necessities and a few comforts: nestled among the items were cuts of fresh meat wrapped in butcher paper, vibrant vegetables that still carried the earthy scent of the garden, and a bundle of fresh herbs, their aromatic presence subtly perfuming the air around them. Beside these, a box of detergent—a mundane yet essential item—sat alongside a carton of milk, chilled and beading with condensation in the warmth of the day. Tucked in the corner of the basket, a bag of rich, ground coffee and a pack of coffee filters promised the comfort of morning rituals yet to come.

As the children ambled along behind him, their voices a soft murmur of day's end excitement, John's gaze shifted from the goods in his grasp to the two women. His expression mingled concern with curiosity as he noted the tension between them.

"Everything alright?" he asked, setting the basket down with a gentle thud, the contents giving a soft, rustling reply. His eyes moved attentively between Mary and Barbara, seeking to understand the undercurrents of their exchange.

Mary forced a smile, her eyes meeting Barbara's. "Yes, everything's fine. Just catching up."

Barbara returned the smile, though it didn't reach her eyes. "You folks have a good evening. And remember what I said, Mary. Get home before dark."

They gathered their groceries and headed to the local pizza parlor for dinner. The children buzzed with excitement, oblivious to the tension between their parents. The smell of freshly baked pizza filled the air, and for a moment, the normalcy was a balm to Mary's frayed nerves.

Sowing The Seeds

As they sat at a small table, sharing a pizza, John tried to lighten the mood. "So, what's the plan for tomorrow? Maybe a hike or a picnic?"

Mary's eyes flicked to the window, the sky beginning to darken. "Let's just take it one day at a time, okay?"

John nodded, sensing her unease. "Of course."

After dinner, John decided to spoil the kids with a treat, stopping to buy ice cream for everyone. The joyful banter and bright smiles from Ben and Emma, as they chose their flavors, brought a momentary lift to the evening, their delight momentarily pushing aside the heavier atmosphere that had settled around the family.

As they strolled back to the car, the fading light casting long shadows across the parking lot, Mary's sense of nervousness returned. Despite the laughter and chatter of her family, she couldn't escape the prickling sensation of being watched, the chilling echo of Barbara's words reverberating in her mind.

John, sensing Mary's tension as they approached the car, tried to keep the atmosphere light. "Who knew choosing between chocolate and vanilla could be such a serious business, eh?" he joked, managing a smile as he packed the leftover ice cream into the ice chest in the back of the car.

Mary forced a smile, appreciating John's effort. "Yeah, it's the decision of the century for them," she replied, her tone light but distracted.

They all piled back into the car, with John glancing around subtly, picking up on Mary's discomfort. "Everything alright?" he asked quietly, as he started the engine.

Mary nodded, not wanting to worry the kids. "Yes, just tired, I guess," she murmured, her eyes scanning the tree line one last time as John drove them away from the ice cream shop and back towards the uncertainty waiting at home.

The drive home was quiet, and the tension was high. The sun began to dip back behind the trees, the twilight deepening into night. Mary clutched John's hand, her knuckles white, her mind repeating the clerk's words like a mantra.

The sun had set by the time the Harper family returned home, the house enveloped in the tail end of dusk as they carried their groceries inside. Mary's heart raced as she glanced at the darkened tree line, the ominous quiet of the forest unrelenting. She forced herself to take a deep breath and followed John and the kids into the house.

Inside, the living room radiated a warm glow from the lamps, casting a soft, inviting light across the walls, which helped temper the unsettling atmosphere of the day. John, seeking to dispel the tension, turned to Mary and the kids with a smile, trying to inject some normalcy into the evening. Mary watched him, her mind a whirl of confusion—torn between the rational explanation of possible mold causing their experiences and Barbara's ominous suggestions that something deeper was amiss with their new home.

"How about we pick out a movie to watch together?" he suggested, his voice deliberately cheerful. "Something light, maybe a comedy, to end the day on a better note." He hoped the familiar ritual of family movie night might restore a sense of normalcy, however fleeting.

Mary tried to settle into the calm evening, although a residual unease continued to shadow her thoughts.

"I don't know, Dad, we've already watched all the movies," Emma complained, her voice tinged with the restlessness of a typical teenager. "I'd rather just go upstairs and chat with my friends."

John prepared for this, smiled, and pulled a DVD from his bag, a surprise he had picked up from the store. "What about this? 'Zombies.' It's got cheerleaders in it—thought you might enjoy it," he said, winking at her.

Emma's eyes lit up as she recognized one of her favorites, a guilty pleasure. "Okay, that one I'll watch!" she exclaimed, her earlier reluctance forgotten.

Ben, overhearing the excitement, couldn't resist teasing his sister. He put on an exaggerated valley girl accent, "Like, totally let's watch some cheerleaders fight zombies!" His playful mimicry drew a laugh from Emma and even coaxed a small smile from Mary.

As John loaded the Blu-ray disc into the player and snapped the door shut, the family arranged themselves on the couch. The children snuggled in, their laughter and playful banter filling the room with a light-hearted energy. Emma and Ben were completely absorbed, eagerly anticipating the start of their favorite zombie cheerleader movie.

Mary attempted to relax alongside her family, trying to immerse herself in the cheerful routine that the movie night brought. Yet, despite the familiar comfort of the living room and the joyous sounds of her children, a creeping sense of nervousness wound its way through her thoughts. As the screen lit up, casting dancing lights and shadows across the room, Mary couldn't help but feel a disconnect from the scene of domestic bliss. Her gaze often drifted to the dim corners of the room or the slightly ajar doorway, as if expecting to catch sight of something—or some-one—peering in.

While John and the kids laughed at a particularly silly scene, Mary's laughter was forced, her smiles fleeting. She felt an inexplicable chill, as though a cold draft had brushed against her skin, even though the windows were closed. The more she tried to focus on the movie, the more her mind raced, haunted by the unnerving incidents of the past days, making her feel isolated in her own home.

As the movie played, the house grew eerily quiet. The wind outside had died down, and even the usual nighttime sounds seemed to have vanished. The oppressive silence pressed in on Mary once again, her nerves fraying with each passing moment.

Then, faintly at first, the whistling began. It was the same haunting melody, rising and falling in a sinister cadence. Mary's heart pounded in her chest, and she gripped the edge of the couch, her knuckles white.

"Do you hear that?" she whispered, her voice trembling.

John glanced at her, his brow furrowed. "Sweets, it's just your imagination. Try to relax."

But Mary couldn't relax. The whistling grew louder, more insistent, wrapping around her mind like a vice. She clutched her head, her breath coming in short gasps. And then, through the whistling, she heard it—a soft, insidious whisper.

"Mary... Mary..."

Her eyes widened in terror. "No, I didn't," she whispered, her voice shaking. "No, I didn't."

The soft, eerie whistle pierced the evening calm, sending a chill down John's spine as he heard it too, but he remained steadfast, trying to be the pillar of calm for his family. Mary clutched at her chest, her breath quickening as the sound filled the room. Emma and Ben huddled closer, their eyes wide with fear, sensing the tension in the air.

"It's just the wind, kids," John murmured, even as his voice betrayed his anxiety. "There's nothing to worry about." But as he moved towards the window to reassure himself as much as his family, the whistling grew louder, more melodic, yet chilling.

Peering out, John's eyes widened in disbelief. There, in front of the house, the two girls Mary said she had seen just yesterday paced back and forth. Their movements were eerie, almost mechanical, as they whistled a haunting tune. Suddenly, they took each other's hands and began skipping in a circle, singing in a lilting, creepy rhyme:

"Father's calling us to play, Happiness is on its way."

Mary, drawn by the commotion, joined John at the window, her face pale as she watched the scene unfold. Emma and Ben came up behind, clinging to each other, their faces etched with fright.

"Do you believe me now, babe?" Mary's voice was a mix of vindication and fear.

John turned to look at her, his face ashen, his usual skepticism washed away by the unfolding nightmare. "I... I don't know what to believe anymore," he admitted, shaken.

The girls continued their chilling dance, their voices weaving through the night air:

"Round and round, we dance and sway, Father's joy is here to stay."

As the children whimpered, clinging to their parents, the whispered enticements from outside grew more insistent, targeting Mary with eerie precision. "Mary... come to us..."

"No, I didn't. No, I didn't," Mary repeated frantically, trying to shut out the voices.

John wrapped his arms around his family, his eyes fixed on the haunting figures outside. The reality of their situation was undeniable, and terror gripped his heart as he realized the full extent of their peril.

"Those are the two girls I saw yesterday when Ben ran out of the car. Those are them," Mary said, her voice trembling with urgency as she pointed out the window at the eerie figures.

"But Mary, none of that happened yesterday. This can't be happening," John replied, his voice a mixture of disbelief and denial, struggling to reconcile the reality before his eyes with the normality he desperately clung to.

"It is happening, babe. And we can't just blame this on mold," Mary insisted, her voice rising in frustration.

"There's no way we could all be having the same hallucinations at the same time. It just doesn't make sense."

Her assertion was firm, underlined by the very real and shared experience they were witnessing now. What Mary had seen with Ben the night before was not a dream but a forewarning—a glimpse of the chilling reality that was now unfolding right before their eyes. This moment, with the two girls outside, was undeniably real, a sinister echo of her premonition that brought an ominous clarity to their situation.

"Kids, upstairs, now!" John's voice cracked with urgency, a stark contrast to his usual calm demeanor. "Lock your doors and stay there until I come get you."

Emma and Ben exchanged a frightened glance before scrambling towards the stairs, their movements hurried and shaky. "Hurry!" John barked as he watched them disappear around the corner.

Meanwhile, outside, the two girls began to intensify their antics, their movements growing wilder. They started spinning faster, their singsong voices rising into the night. Suddenly, in a blink, they vanished, leaving behind an eerie silence that seemed to press against the windows.

The sudden disappearance of the girls sent a surge of panic through John. He turned back to Mary, who was pale and visibly shaking. "They're gone," he muttered, his voice barely a whisper.

Mary, her eyes wide with terror, barely heard him. "It's starting again—the whistling, the whispers. They're calling out, trying to lure us..." Her voice was frantic, her fear palpable in the dim light of the living room.

John's instinct to protect his family kicked in as he moved swiftly to check the locks on the doors and windows, his actions quick and deliberate. "We need to stay together, keep calm," he said over his shoulder, trying to infuse his voice with confidence he didn't feel.

Just then, a soft but clear whistling filled the house, as if the sound were winding its way through every room, every crack. The atmosphere tensed, the earlier chaos outside having seeped into their home.

"John!" Mary's voice was a sharp cry, snapping him out of his focus. He turned to see her pointing towards the hallway, her hand trembling. "There, did you see that? Shadows, moving!"

John squinted into the darkened hallway, seeing nothing but feeling an undeniable chill that made the hairs on his neck stand. "Okay, okay. I didn't see it, but I believe something strange is happening. Let's stick together, and we'll get through this. Maybe it's time we called someone—"

Before he could finish, a loud thud resonated from upstairs, cutting him off. Emma's terrified scream followed, slicing through the tense air.

"Mom! Dad!" her voice wailed from the upper floor.

Without a second thought, John and Mary rushed towards the staircase, hearts pounding, each step fueled by a mix of dread and the desperate need to protect their children. Whatever was happening in their home was no longer just a haunting outside—it had invited itself in.

John and Mary raced up the stairs, their hearts thudding in their chests, each step echoing ominously through the house. As they reached the top, they found Emma standing in the doorway of Ben's room, her face pale with shock, her eyes wide with fear.

Inside the room, Ben was on the floor, his body convulsing in violent spasms, an eerie, continuous whistle escaping his lips. The sound was chilling, otherworldly, as if it were not entirely his own.

"Ben!" Mary cried out, her voice breaking with panic as she rushed to her son's side. John swiftly scooped Ben up, his arms firm around the boy, and gently laid him on the bed. Ben's body continued to shake, the whistling growing louder, more desperate.

"Call 911, Mary!" John shouted, his voice laced with urgency as he held Ben, trying to stabilize him.

Mary fumbled with her phone, her hands trembling as she dialed the emergency number. She held the phone to her ear, her expression turning from panic to dismay as she realized the line was dead. "It's not working, dammit! The line's dead!" she exclaimed, the desperation in her voice rising.

John looked around the room frantically, his mind racing for alternatives. "Check your cell, maybe it's just the landline!"

Mary quickly pulled out her cell phone from her pocket, her fingers hastily unlocking it and dialing again. She held her breath, hoping for a ring, but her face fell as she met the same dead silence. "Nothing! There's no signal at all!"

John's gaze returned to Ben, whose convulsions had begun to subside, leaving him lying eerily still on the bed, the whistling fading into a haunting, intermittent echo. He turned to Mary, his eyes conveying a mix of fear and resolve. "We're on our own, then. We need to figure out what's happening to him, fast."

Mary nodded, her eyes brimming with tears as she looked down at Ben, then back at John. "What do we do? What can we do?"

"We have to keep him stable and figure out what triggered this," John replied, his voice steady despite the chaos swirling around them. "We'll start by keeping him calm and quiet. Watch him closely. I'll go get some water and a wet cloth. We need to keep him cool."

As John hurried out of the room to fetch the supplies, Mary sat by Ben's side, her hand gently stroking his forehead, whispering soothing words to her son, her mind racing with fear but determined to keep her terror at bay for the sake of her family. Meanwhile, the shadows seemed to press closer around the edges of the room, as if drawn to the vulnerability and fear permeating the air.

The whistling continued and seemed to seep into the walls around them. Mary closed her eyes, and covered her ears trying to block out the sound, but it only grew louder, more insistent.

"Mary... come to us..."

"No, I didn't. No, I didn't," she whispered, her voice breaking.

John returned to Ben's room with a bowl of cold water and a cloth. He dipped the cloth into the water, wrung it out slightly, and gently placed it on Ben's forehead, who now lay quiet and still on the bed, his breathing had evened out into a peaceful rhythm. The eerie whistling had ceased, and for a moment, the room was filled with a tense silence, broken only by the soft, rhythmic sounds of Ben's breaths.

Turning his attention to Emma, who stood by the doorway, her eyes wide and filled with unshed tears, John beckoned her closer. "Come here, Emma," he said gently, and she approached, hesitantly. He wrapped an arm around her shoulders, pulling her into a reassuring hug. "It's going to be okay," he murmured, his voice soothing. "Ben's going to be fine now, see? He's resting, just like he should."

Emma nodded against his chest, her body relaxing slightly as she took comfort in her father's presence. John felt her exhale deeply, her earlier panic subsiding into quiet worry.

As Emma calmed down, John's gaze shifted back to Mary, who sat beside Ben, her eyes fixed on her son with an intensity that spoke volumes of her fear. Despite the calm that had settled over the children, Mary's expression remained fraught with anxiety. Her hands were clasped tightly in her lap, and she seemed to be murmuring quietly to herself, lost in her thoughts.

"Honey," John started, his tone cautious as he approached her. "Ben's stable now, and Emma's calmed down. We're going to get through this." He paused, searching for the right words to reassure her further. "I still think this could be something environmental, like the mold. Once we get that checked and cleared up, I'm sure things will start to make more sense."

Mary turned to look at him, her eyes reflecting a turmoil that hadn't eased with Ben's recovery. "I hope you're right," she replied, her voice low and weary. "But what I heard, what I saw... It felt too real, too malicious to be just... mold."

John nodded, understanding her skepticism yet clinging to his rational explanations as a lifeline in the chaos. "We'll get everything checked out," he reassured her, his voice firm. "For now, let's just keep an eye on the kids and try to get some rest ourselves. We need to stay strong for them."

As John helped Mary to her feet, he felt the weight of responsibility pressing down on him. Despite his attempts to rationalize the situation, a part of him couldn't dismiss Mary's fears outright. He glanced around the dimly lit room, feeling a chill that seemed unrelated to the night air. Whether it was mold or something more sinister, he knew the coming days would be crucial in uncovering the truth behind the harrowing events that had shaken their family to its core.

The night stretched on, the oppressive atmosphere growing thicker, more suffocating. The whistling and whispers filled the house, an unrelenting reminder of the malevolent presence that haunted them. As the darkness deepened, Mary felt herself slipping further into the grip of madness, her sanity fraying like a delicate thread.

Outside, the forest stood silent and watchful, its secrets hidden in the shadows. The house, once a sanctuary, had become a prison, trapping the Harpers in a nightmare from which there seemed to be no escape. And as the whistling continued, Mary knew what would come next.

INTO THE WOODS

John held Mary tightly, trying to calm her trembling form. The oppressive atmosphere in the house seemed to be mocking Mary. The whistling echoed in Mary's ears. Desperate to break the spell, John gently released her.

"I'll get you some water," he said, his voice steady. "Stay right here."

As John disappeared into the kitchen, Mary attempted to anchor herself to the normalcy of the family movie night. Yet, despite the familiar, cheerful scenes unfolding on the TV, a persistent whistling seeped into the edges of her consciousness, insidious and relentless. It started as a faint, distant sound, barely noticeable over the dialogue and soundtrack of the film, but it gradually grew into an all-encompassing force, impossible to ignore.

The whistling wound its way through her mind like a sinister vine, twisting around her thoughts and tightening with each eerie note. It was as if the sound bore an evil will, intent on suffocating her sanity, plucking at the strings of her perception with chilling precision. Each whistle seemed to echo from the dark corners of the room, rebounding off the walls to fill the space with its disturbing presence.

Mary's heart raced; her palms became clammy as she gripped the armrest of the sofa. The cheerful light from the TV screen now seemed harshly out of place against the darkening corners of her mind where shadows danced to the tune of the whistling. The sound was no longer just a noise—it felt alive, a spectral entity that feasted on her growing dread.

Her eyes darted around the room, half-expecting to catch a glimpse of some ghastly apparition materializing with each whistle. Her breathing grew shallow, each inhale sharp and each exhale quivering with fear. The more she tried to pull herself back to the reality of her living room, the deeper she felt dragged into the abyss of her terror.

The movie's laughter and lighthearted banter were all but gone, muffled by the storm of her fear. Mary felt isolated as if the whistling had enveloped her in a bubble, cutting her off from her family, from safety. In her mind, the whistling morphed into a mocking taunt, a reminder that something wicked lurked just beyond the veil of her understanding, waiting, watching, biding its time.

Then, through the whistling, she heard it again—the soft, insidious whisper.

"Mary... Mary..."

Her heart pounded. "No, I didn't," she whispered, her voice shaking. "No, I didn't."

John winced as he scrubbed at a glass a bit too harshly and it shattered in his hand, the sudden, sharp crack echoing through the kitchen. Small shards of glass bit into his skin, and blood immediately began to well up, vivid and startling against his skin. "Damn it," he cursed under his breath, pain and frustration flaring as he quickly grabbed a washcloth from the drawer to press against the wound.

As he wrapped the fabric tightly around his hand, stifling the flow of blood, he muttered to himself, *What the hell am I supposed to do here?* The sight of his own blood mingling with water in the sink was a harsh reminder of the stress they were all under. *She's losing it, and I'm here playing nurse, fuck, am I losing it too... are we all losing it.* He grumbled, his voice a mix of worry and exasperation.

Turning the tap back on to wash away the blood, he watched the water swirl down the drain, a mix of frustration and compassion swirling within him as well. *I've got to pull it together, Mary needs me,* he thought aloud, the concern in his voice palpable. *But, shit, watching everyone fall apart like this... it's tearing me up.*

Carefully, John reached for a new glass with his good hand, filled it, and took a moment to collect himself, his breathing deep and steady to manage the pain and stress. *All right, John, just get through this night,* he whispered to himself, steeling his resolve as he prepared to return to Mary.

Mary's eyes drifted upwards towards the stairs, and she stopped cold. There, at the top, stood Ben, his gaze fixed on her with a piercing, almost unnatural intensity. His figure appeared ethereal, more like a wraith than her flesh-and-blood son. It was as if she was seeing a mirage, a spectral version of Ben, caught somewhere between reality and a haunting premonition.

"Mom, let's go play in the woods. Race me there," he said, his voice strangely devoid of emotion.

Before Mary could react, Ben turned and sprinted down the stairs, his footsteps echoing through the house. He flung the front door open and dashed outside.

"B-Ben, no! Stop!" Mary screamed, bolting from the couch. She ran after him, her heart pounding in her chest.

John heard the commotion from the kitchen and rushed out, the glass of water forgotten. The front door was wide open, and Mary was nowhere to be seen. Panic surged through him as he ran to the door, his eyes scanning the dark yard.

"Mary!" he shouted, his voice echoing in the still night.

He saw Mary running towards the woods, her silhouette barely visible against the thick tree line. Before he could call out again, she disappeared into the shadows. Fear clawing at his insides, John grabbed a flashlight and sprinted after her.

The beam of the flashlight cut through the darkness, illuminating the twisted branches and dense undergrowth. John's breath came in ragged gasps as he plunged into the forest, the trees closing in around him.

"Mary! Where are you?" John yelled; his voice hoarse with desperation.

He heard a faint whimpering up ahead, barely audible over his heavy breathing. John pushed through the underbrush, the flashlight beam dancing wildly. He stumbled upon Mary, curled in the fetal position on the forest floor, her body shaking with sobs.

"Mary," he breathed, dropping to his knees beside her. "Sweetheart, it's okay. I'm here."

She looked up at him, her eyes filled with terror and confusion. "Ben... he was here. He wanted to play in the woods. I... I saw him. I tried to catch him but it was too late. John, he jumped into that hole over there."

John rushed over in the direction that Mary was pointing and he came to a deep hole. It looked like it was where one of the Mica mines may have collapsed. John shined his flashlight down into the hole but the beam of light did not reach the bottom.

"Are you sure you saw him?" John said with a concerned look.

"Babe, I don't, ugh...I d-don't fucking know anymore. I swear I saw him. I saw our sweet angel race out of the house and so I chased after him. I followed him to this damn clearing and h-he stopped before that hole right there and looked back at me. Do you know what he said? He fucking said, it's time for me to go momma, and then he jumped!"

John struggled to reconcile the situation with Mary's escalating panic. Her fragile state made it difficult for him to take her claims at face value.

"I don't think Ben would just wander off like that. Let's head back to the house so I can grab a brighter flashlight. While we're there, I'll check his room to make sure he's still in bed," John suggested, trying to inject a note of rationality into the conversation.

Mary's voice trembled with urgency; her eyes wide with fear. "O-okay, but I'm telling you, he-he's down in that hole! We need to call someone! We need to save him!"

Her plea echoed in the cool night air, laden with a mother's desperation. The raw emotion in her voice made it clear that this was more than mere anxiety; it was a visceral fear for her son's safety.

John wrapped his arms around her, pulling her close. ", Ben is at home. You're just... you're confused. Let's get back to the house."

Mary gripped John tightly, her body shaking as she fought to make him understand. "No, John, it was real. He was here. He was right here! I saw him, but he looked... he looked like a ghost. It was Ben. I know how this sounds, John, I do, but please, please believe me. Forget the mold for a second. We can't just write everything off as goddamn mold! And the two girls we saw... that was real, not a hallucination! I know it's hard to accept, and I'm struggling too, but we have to admit that something deeply wrong is happening here."

John helped Mary to her feet, his hand gripping her arm firmly to steady her. "We'll figure this out Mary, but we really should get back to the house. It's not safe out here," he said, his voice steady despite the urgency of the situation.

He glanced around the dense forest, then added somewhat hastily, "I mean, I think I saw some bear tracks not too far from here just the other day. We really shouldn't be out here like this, not equipped for... you know, bears and stuff."

Though in reality, John hadn't seen any bear tracks, the fabrication was a quick attempt to underscore the need for safety and to provide a plausible reason to persuade Mary to return to the house, hoping it would help calm her as they made their way back.

As they made their way back through the forest, the whistling seemed to recede in Mary's mind, replaced by the rustling of leaves and the distant cries of nocturnal animals. The oppressive weight of the forest pressed down on them, making each step feel like a struggle.

Finally, they emerged from the tree line, the house a dark silhouette against the night sky. John led Mary inside, locking the door behind them. He guided her to the couch, wrapping a blanket around her shoulders.

"Stay here. I'll go check on the kids and then I'll get that water," he said softly, his voice filled with concern.

Mary nodded, her eyes distant and haunted. "Don't leave me, John. Please!"

"I'll be right back," he promised, hurrying up the stairs. John hollered back down to Mary who was now slowly swaying back and forth with her palms pressed against her eyes.

"Mary!" John yelled a little louder, trying to not wake the children.

She moved her head in the direction of John's voice, her eyes still covered. "He's gone, isn't he?"

"Both Emma and Ben are fast asleep Mary. You need to stop with this crap Mary. You're going to give me a damn heart attack."

John trudged back down the stairs, his frustration boiling over into anger. He entered the kitchen, deliberately avoiding looking at Mary, who was deep in the throes of what seemed like a mental breakdown. The glass of water he had filled earlier waited on the counter, the light flickering overhead, casting uneasy shadows.

John paced back and forth, his mind a turbulent mix of anger and confusion. Each echo of Mary's claims hammered against the walls of his logic, forcing him to confront a reality he could neither understand nor control. "What the hell is happening to us?" he muttered under his breath, his voice laced with a bitterness he couldn't suppress. "Is Mary losing her mind, or is there really something more going on here?"

He grabbed a glass of water, his hand shaking slightly as he filled it, his grip so tight it seemed he might shatter yet another glass. "Am I supposed to just keep soothing her?" he thought, his frustration mounting with each passing moment. "How can I keep doing this when I don't even understand what I'm fighting against?"

Turning sharply, he carried the glass back to where Mary was waiting, his steps heavy, his heart racing with a mix of dread and defiance. The tension between them had grown palpable, fed by his mounting hostility and her persistent fears. It was as if Harold's shadowy influence was weaving its way into their lives, pulling at the seams of their sanity.

John's demeanor had shifted; once the steady cornerstone of their family, he now found himself lashing out, unable to reconcile the man he was with the man he was becoming. Deep down, he sensed the truth in Mary's frantic words, having witnessed the inexplicable himself, yet his denial formed a barrier he wasn't ready to tear down.

As he approached Mary, the look in his eyes was a turbulent mix of conflict and capitulation. "We need to get to the bottom of this," he said, his voice harsher than he intended. "But Mary, we need to handle this rationally. We can't let fear take over."

His words, meant to fortify, instead felt like accusations, adding weight to the already heavy air. Harold's plan, unseen but deeply felt, was working—sowing discord and fear, driving a wedge through the heart of their family. As John handed Mary the glass, his hands were not just offering sustenance but also signaling a truce he hoped they could keep, even as the darkness around them deepened.

Returning to the living room, John handed Mary the glass of water and sat beside her, his arm around her shoulders. "Drink this. It will help."

Mary's hands shook as she raised the glass to her lips, taking small, cautious sips. She sat next to John on the couch, her eyes wide with confusion and fear, desperately seeking his gaze for some semblance of stability amidst the turmoil within her mind. "Babe, I'm fucking losing it," she whispered, her voice laced with desperation. "I can't tell what's real and what's not anymore!"

John pulled Mary close, his arms tight around her as they sank into the cushions. His voice was soft yet strained as he lifted her chin, forcing her to meet his gaze. "Hey, look at me," he said, a tinge of frustration seeping through his attempt at gentleness. "You've got to pull yourself together, Mary. This isn't like you." His words were meant to comfort, but they carried an underlying edge of exasperation at the surreal turn their lives had taken.

As they sat together, the space around them felt both comforting and constrictive, a silent witness to their struggle. John could feel Mary's heartbeat racing, her breath uneven against his chest. "We've handled tough times before, right?" he continued, his voice soft yet filled with a quiet strength. "We'll handle this one too. Just stay with me. We'll get through this day by day."

Mary nodded, a fragile smile breaking through her worry as she leaned into his embrace, letting his steady presence soothe her turbulent thoughts. Their shared resolve filled the space, mingling with the soft rustle of the curtains and the low hum of the TV in the background, where the closing credits of their zombie movie scrolled silently across the screen—a subtle reminder that life, with all its unpredictability, still moved forward around them.

Mary looked over at John frantically. "I'm not crazy, right? You heard the whistling too."

John felt the urge to agree with Mary, to acknowledge the surreal horrors they'd all witnessed. It would simplify everything, and ease the growing tension. Yet, something within him resisted, a persistent whisper that seemed to crawl into his thoughts, urging him to dismiss it all as delusions.

As he looked into Mary's anxious eyes, part of him ached to reassure her, to join her in this fight against the unknown. But this intrusive voice, cold and manipulative, coiled tighter around his reasoning, pushing him to contradict, to invalidate her experiences. It was as though some unseen force was deliberately trying to drive a wedge between them, to isolate Mary and push her deeper into despair.

Each time John opened his mouth to speak, the words that came out were not of comfort but of skepticism and doubt. "Mary, we need to think logically about this," he found himself saying, his tone more detached than he intended. "You're letting your fear get the best of you. Maybe it's stress, or maybe we're just not used to the new house yet."

The look of hurt that flashed across Mary's face was like a punch to his gut. He knew he was adding to her turmoil, yet he felt powerless to stop it. This internal battle left him feeling like a stranger in his own body, as if he were watching himself from the sidelines, unable to regain control.

As he continued to dismiss her claims, the atmosphere in the room thickened with tension and despair. The unseen influence seemed pleased with the discord it sowed, feeding off their growing estrangement. John hated the rift that was forming between them, yet he couldn't seem to bridge it, trapped by the whispering voice that seemed hell-bent on plunging Mary further into madness.

"I'm telling you, sweetheart, it's just the new noises of the house. You've lived most of your life in the city, and these things can take time to get used to. I think you're just exhausted and stressed out. A couple of days of good rest will have you feeling a lot better."

As the night stretched on, the whistling remained silent, but the memory of its haunting melody lingered in Mary's mind. The dark presence around the house seemed to retreat, but she knew it was still there, waiting for the next opportunity to strike.

In the dim light of the living room, shadows stretched and twisted into more sinister shapes, each one subtly hinting at the arduous hours still to unfold. The room was steeped in a heavy stillness, broken only by the occasional creaks of the timeworn house, which sounded like subdued sighs from an old, weary spirit.

John held Mary close, her trembling gradually easing under the weight of exhaustion. Despite the superficial calm, there was a palpable tension in the air, as if the house itself was bracing for what was to come. Upstairs, the children were nestled in their beds, cloaked in a deceptive tranquility. For a fleeting moment, it seemed they might escape into rest.

However, as shadows deepened and the clock ticked relentlessly forward, the encroaching darkness began to press closer against the windows, the night air thick with the unsaid and unseen. The promise of peace was slowly overshadowed by the growing presence of the night, each passing hour drawing the family closer to the unseen edges of reality that lingered just out of sight.

Hours later, as the moon climbed higher in the sky, Ben stirred in his bed. His eyes opened slowly, glassy and vacant, reflecting the pale moonlight filtering through the window. He sat up, his movements stiff and mechanical, and swung his legs over the side of the bed.

Without making a sound, Ben slipped out of his room and padded down the hallway. His small feet barely made a whisper against the wooden floorboards as he approached the staircase. At the top of the stairs, he paused, staring down into the living room where his parents were huddled together on the couch.

John had fallen asleep, his head resting against the back of the couch. Mary, though still awake, was lost in her thoughts, her eyes distant and unfocused. Ben's expression remained blank as he watched them, an unsettling stillness in his posture.

Slowly, Ben descended the stairs, his eyes never leaving his parents. He moved with an eerie grace, each step deliberate and silent. When he reached the bottom, he stood for a moment, simply watching them. The shadows seemed to twist and curl around him, almost as if they were alive.

Then, without warning, he began to whistle the same haunting melody that had filled the house only hours earlier. The sound was soft at first, barely audible, but it grew louder, more insistent, echoing through the silent room.

Mary's head snapped up, her heart pounding. "Ben? What are you doing?"

Ben's gaze met Mary's, but it was empty, devoid of any warmth or recognition. The haunting whistle continued, his lips twisting into an unsettling smile as he took a deliberate step toward her. This time, there was no mistaking the solidity of his presence; he wasn't the spectral figure she had seen just hours before. This was unmistakably the real Ben, flesh and blood, standing right in front of her. The stark reality of the situation hit Mary—this was not a hallucination or a dream. Ben was truly there, altered and chillingly real.

"Ben, stop it. You're scaring me," Mary said, her voice trembling.

John stirred beside her, waking from his uneasy sleep. "What's going on?"

Mary's eyes were wide with fear. "It's Ben. He's... whistling that song again."

John turned to look at his son, a cold dread settling over him. "Ben, come here, buddy. Let's get you back to bed."

But Ben didn't move. Instead, he began to speak, his voice a strange, echoing whisper. "Mommy, Daddy, come play with me in the woods. It's fun in the woods. We'll be happy there."

Mary's breath caught in her throat. "Ben, stop it. This isn't funny."

Ben's smile widened; his eyes gleaming with an unnatural light. "Come with me. Come play."

John stood, his heart racing. "Ben, that's enough. Come here."

But as he took a step forward, Ben turned and ran towards the front door, his laughter echoing through the house. John and Mary bolted after him, but by the time they reached the door, it was already open, and Ben was sprinting towards the woods.

"Ben, no!" Mary screamed, running after him. "Come back!"

John grabbed the flashlight he still had in his pocket after chasing Mary earlier in the evening and followed, his fear morphing into a desperate determination. The beam of light cut through the darkness, but Ben was already disappearing into the thick tree line.

"Wait!" John shouted, but she was already gone, her figure swallowed by the shadows of the forest.

He plunged into the woods after them, the flashlight beam bouncing wildly. The whistling started again, louder and more frenzied, mingling with Ben's eerie laughter. John needed to reach them both before they got too close to the clearing.

"Ben! Mary!" John called; his voice ragged.

He could hear Mary ahead, her sobs and frantic pleas mingling with the eerie whistling of the wind. Pushing through the dense undergrowth, John finally caught sight of her. Mary was kneeling on the ground, her hands clutching the earth as if trying to hold onto reality itself, her body trembling with each sob.

"Babe, it's happening again!" she cried out as he approached. Her eyes were wide with terror, fixed on a spot just beyond the trees. "Hurry, we have to get Ben before... before he jumps into that hole!" Her voice cracked under the strain, urgency propelling her words.

"Mary!" John dropped to his knees beside her, his heart pounding. "Where's Ben? What happened?"

Mary looked up at him, her eyes wild with terror. "He... he was right here. He wanted me to follow him. He said... he said we'd be happy in the woods."

John's blood ran cold. "Stay here. I'll find him."

He stood, the flashlight beam sweeping across the dark forest. The whistling seemed to come from all directions, wrapping around him, and pulling him deeper into the trees.

"Ben! Where are you?" he shouted, his voice echoing through the night.

And then, he saw him. Ben stood a few yards away, his back to John, swaying slightly as if caught in the rhythm of the eerie whistling that filled the air. John's emotions surged—a mix of relief at seeing his son and rising anger toward Mary, whose erratic behavior he felt was exacerbating their crisis. Despite his frustration, he knew he needed to remain composed to coax Ben back from the edge of the forest.

John moved closer, trying to steady his breath and calm the tempest inside him. With each careful step, he prepared to speak gently to Ben, to draw him away from the strange, hypnotic sway of the whistling without startling him.

"Ben, come back. Let's go home."

BEN

Ben turned slowly to face John, and when their eyes met, there was a haunting emptiness in Ben's stare that struck a cold fear into John's heart. His son's eyes, normally warm and lively, now seemed to harbor a chilling void, as if something else was looking out from behind them. Ben's smile then spread across his face, unnatural and unsettling, twisting what should have been a comforting gesture into something sinister. This eerie transformation made John's skin crawl, the forest around them suddenly feeling more oppressive, as if the shadows themselves were closing in.

"Come play with me, Daddy," Ben said, his voice carrying a disturbingly soft and hollow tone. "Come play in the woods."

John reached out, but before he could grab him, Ben turned and ran deeper into the forest, disappearing into the darkness. John chased after him, his fear driving him forward, but the trees seemed to close in around him, the whistling growing louder, more frantic.

John's heart pounded as he stumbled through the dense underbrush, each step more desperate than the last. The beam from his flashlight, now dim and flickering as the batteries waned. His breaths came in ragged gasps, heavy with the cold air of the night and thick with panic. Bursting into a large clearing, he halted abruptly, his eyes widening in disbelief.

There, in the center of the moonlit clearing, stood Ben. His small figure was creepily illuminated by the soft glow of the moon, his eyes unnaturally calm as they locked onto John's with an unsettling intensity.

"Ben, what are you doing out here?" John's voice cracked, the words tumbling out in a mix of relief and terror.

"Dad, it's time for me to go. They want me to go with them," Ben's voice was eerily composed, far too serene for a child in the middle of the woods at night. "Tell Mom and Emma that I love them."

John's heart sank, a surge of fear tightening around it. "What do you mean, Ben? Get over here, now! Enough of these damn games. It's time for bed."

"The whistles are calling me, Dad. I need to go now," Ben said, his voice drifting across the clearing like a cold breeze.

"Ben, no! Stop playing around. It's dangerous out here," John pleaded, his voice a desperate shout in the quiet of the woods.

But Ben turned, his figure receding into the shadows as he moved with purpose towards something unseen. John sprinted forward, his feet barely touching the ground, the terror for his son fueling his speed. He reached the spot where Ben had stood just moments before and found the ominous hole Mary had spoken of—her words, once dismissed as frantic delusions, now echoed in his mind with horrifying clarity.

Was he going insane, or had Mary somehow foreseen this? The thought tormented John as he dropped to his knees beside the hole, the earth cold and unforgiving under his hands. He leaned over, putting his ear close to the dark opening, listening for any sign of Ben. But there was nothing—only the haunting echo of the wind as it whistled through the empty void, mimicking the call that had drawn his son away.

Tears streamed down John's face, each one a mixture of fear, frustration, and a piercing, heart-wrenching helplessness. "Ben!" he shouted into the void, his voice breaking, the sound swallowed by the darkness below.

John cupped his hands around his mouth in an effort to direct his voice down to the bottom, if there even was one. "Ben, are you down there? Can you hear me?"

There was no response. That is when he knew his son was gone and he grabbed onto the tall grass while on his knees and yelled up into the night sky, "What the fuck do you want from us? You son of a bitch, why would you take my son?"

He sat there quietly sobbing for a few minutes before he heard a voice calling out to him desperate and terrified.

"John! Help me! Please!"

Mary stumbled through the underbrush, frantically searching for John and Ben. "John! Ben!" she called, her voice breaking with desperation.

But there was no response. The woods were silent, as the darkness closed in around them. She ran in circles, her heart pounding, her breath coming in short, panicked gasps.

Finally, she gave up, her legs trembling with exhaustion. She made her way back to the house, tears streaming down her face. As she approached the porch, she saw Emma standing there, her eyes wide and unblinking.

"Emma?" Mary whispered, her voice trembling. "What are you doing out here?"

Emma tilted her head, a strange, eerie smile spreading across her face. "Mommy, did you hear the whispers too? They said that I'm next."

She reached out to her daughter, but the world around her seemed to blur and fade. Darkness closed in, and she felt herself slipping away.

WAS IT ALL A NIGHTMARE

M orning light filtered through the curtains, casting a pale glow across the living room. Mary stirred awake, her heart heavy with dread from the events of the previous night. As she turned to her side, she saw John sitting beside her.

John sat motionless on the living room couch, his gaze locked on some unseen point beyond the window, the kind of stare that pierced through the still, heavy air of the room.

"Babe?" Mary's voice was shaky as she approached him, her hand tentatively reaching out to touch his shoulder. He seemed a million miles away, ensnared by a mix of shock and grief.

His reaction was minimal, a slight twitch under her touch. His eyes, unfocused and distant, seemed to replay the night's horrors over and over.

"Babe, what's wrong?" Mary's concern deepened as she sat beside him, her voice tinged with her own rising panic.

It took a moment for John to respond, his eyes slowly meeting hers as if he were dragging himself back from the brink of a dark abyss. When he finally focused on her, Mary gasped at the tears pooling in his eyes—tears she had never seen him shed before. The man who had always been her steadfast support was now crumbling before her.

"Sweetheart," John's voice broke, raw with pain. "He's gone. Our boy... he's gone."

A chill wrapped around Mary's heart. "No, babe, he can't be..."

"He jumped down that mine shaft," John's voice cracked under the weight of his emotion. "He said the whispers called to him. That they needed him."

Mary's heart sank as the horrific reality set in. "Oh God, John..." Tears mirrored his, reflecting a shared desolation.

Mary's voice rose in desperation, her frustration palpable. "Babe, you've heard the whistles too! You've seen those strange girls in the yard. How can you stand there and deny it all?"

John's face twisted with conflict, the internal battle raging within him. Despite what he had witnessed, the voice whispering insidiously in his mind pushed him to contradict, to deny. "Mary, you're the one making all this up.

You're planting these crazy ideas in our heads. It's all in your imagination!"

Mary shook her head, tears brimming in her eyes as she countered with undeniable truth. "No, John. I'm not making this up. You know it. Deep down, you've seen and heard everything just as I have."

But John, caught in the grip of the voice that refused to let him acknowledge the terrifying reality, hardened his stance. "No! It's all coming from you. You're driving us insane with these delusions!" His voice was loud, almost desperate, as if by sheer volume he could drown out both Mary's arguments and the dissonance in his mind.

His denial was vehement, a stark contrast to the doubt and fear that occasionally flickered in his eyes. He turned away, leaving Mary alone with her fears, as he struggled internally with the dissonance between what he truly knew and what he forced himself to believe. The battle within him was intense, the voice in his head crafting a reality far removed from the one unfolding around them, forcing him to reject the truth that lay plainly before his eyes.

John's moment of clarity was fleeting, a brief glimpse of the man he truly was before the dark influence clouded his thoughts. He approached Mary, his demeanor softened by the genuine fear and confusion he felt. "Mary, I've seen it too—all of it. But there's this voice in my head, pushing me, twisting my thoughts, making me say things I don't mean," he confessed, his voice strained with the effort of fighting against the unseen force.

Mary listened, hope flickering in her eyes as John continued, "It's like I'm not in control sometimes. I see and hear the same horrors you do, and I know something's terribly wrong, but..."

His voice trailed off, and his expression darkened once again, the momentary clarity giving way to a resurgence of the hostile influence. "But maybe it is your fault! Maybe you brought this on us, on Ben!" His words lashed out, sharp and accusatory, driven by the malignant whispers that refused to release their grip on him.

Mary stepped back, her heart sinking as she watched the confusion and anger war with each other across John's features. She recognized the torment he was undergoing, caught between reality and the manipulation of the dark presence in their home. Choosing not to provoke him further, she remained silent, her decision born of both love and fear as she watched the crazed, conflicted look in John's eyes deepen.

She knew then that pressing the issue could push John further into the shadows that seemed to ensnare his mind. With a heavy heart, Mary nodded slowly, maintaining her composure. "Okay, babe," she said quietly, her voice steady despite the turmoil she felt. "We'll talk when you're ready."

John's expression flickered with a mix of relief and residual suspicion as he turned away, leaving Mary to ponder their next steps alone. The house felt heavier, charged with an unseen malevolence that seemed to thrive on their discord. Mary knew the road ahead would be treacherous, but she also knew she had to find a way to reach John again, to pull him back from the brink before the darkness consumed him entirely.

"Did I faint when we came out of the woods?" Mary suddenly asked, piecing memories together.

"When I came out... I found you on the ground. Emma was just standing there, frozen," John explained, the memory surfacing like a bad dream. "I carried you to the couch. Then I tried to call the police, but the line was dead. I even tried to drive into town, but the damn car wouldn't start."

The weight of their grim reality settled heavily in the room, pressing down with a suffocating mix of grief, guilt, and unresolved fear.

Mary nodded; her throat tight with sorrow. She knew they had to protect Emma from the horrifying truth of what had happened to her brother.

John reached for her hand, squeezing it tightly. "I'll try and call the sheriff again. We need to... we need to find out what's down there. Maybe there's something... maybe Ben's down there, trapped."

Mary nodded again; her mind numb with shock. She leaned over and held John tightly, both seeking solace in each other's embrace.

Outside, the morning continued its slow march, oblivious to the tragedy that had unfolded just a few short hours ago. But inside, John and Mary's world had been shattered irreparably, leaving behind only echoes of a once-happy family.

As John made the call, Mary sat by his side, her eyes fixed on a family photo on the nightstand—a snapshot of happier times, before the darkness had come to claim their lives. She whispered a silent prayer, hoping that, somehow, they would find peace amidst the chaos that now surrounded them.

The weak morning sunlight struggled through the dense canopy as Sheriff Anderson made his way toward John and Mary, his boots crunching softly on the leaf-littered ground. The atmosphere was heavy with an unspoken dread as they approached the old mineshaft, its dark opening yawning ominously in the forest clearing.

Sheriff Anderson, his face etched with years of seeing too much, met John and Mary's anxious eyes with a solemn nod. "We're going to take a look down there," he declared, his voice firm yet carrying an undercurrent of caution. His gaze lingered on the abyss for a moment longer than necessary, as if measuring the risk.

A team of deputies, equipped with ropes and lights, soon arrived, their gear clinking in the quiet of the forest. The air tensed as they prepared for the descent, each deputy casting wary glances at the foreboding shaft before them.

Deputy Parker began his descent into the shadowy mineshaft, the creak of his harness punctuating the quiet tension in the air. Below him, the darkness seemed to swell, enveloping his figure as he lowered himself deeper into the abyss. As the rope fed through the equipment, a faint, eerie whistling began to seep into the clearing, chilling and persistent.

Mary clutched John's arm tighter, her eyes wide with rising panic as the whistling grew louder, weaving its way into her consciousness. It was as if the sound itself crawled from the depths of the earth, a sinister call that filled her mind with dark urgencies. *"Cut the rope... let the darkness reclaim what it seeks..."* The words swirled around her, chilling and clear.

At the same moment, Parker, now several feet below, winced, pressing his hand against his helmet as if trying to block out a sudden, painful noise. His discomfort was evident even in the dim light from his helmet lamp, reflecting his struggle against the invasive sound.

Driven by the ghastly commands that haunted her thoughts, Mary's gaze darted frantically. She moved with sudden, detached urgency, lunging towards a nearby - officer. Her hands, acting almost on their own accord, snatched a knife from the officer's belt.

"Mary, no!" John's voice broke through the cold air, filled with horror and disbelief.

As if in a trance, Mary screamed, her voice echoing the sounds that had infected her mind. "They must be freed! He must fall!" Her rush toward the rope was desperate, filled with a terrifying conviction.

Deputies quickly intervened, tackling her to the ground just as the knife nearly met its mark. The knife clattered to the ground, and they pinned her down, her body thrashing under their firm grip.

Above them, the team hastily pulled Parker back up as he continued to clutch his head, his face pale and drawn, his expression one of deep terror.

John rushed to help restrain Mary as she fought, influenced by the unseen, chilling force. "What the hell is wrong with you, Mary? You could have killed him!" he cried out, his voice thick with fury and fear.

As Parker was helped out of the shaft, the whistling abruptly ceased, leaving a heavy silence in its wake. The deputies exchanged grave looks; their faces marked by a fear that spoke of old, dark knowledge. The eldest among them stepped forward, his voice grave and filled with a chilling resolve. "If your son is down there, he's with them now, and there is no way in hell any of us are going back down there," he declared, his tone final, echoing ominously through the forest.

The harrowing reality of his words hung heavily in the air as Mary, now subdued, lay limp in John's arms, her face a portrait of horror and disbelief. The clearing was enveloped in a tense, oppressive silence, a foreboding stillness that settled on everyone present.

The sheriff's voice continued, a distant hum as Mary fought back tears. "We'll continue to search, expand the perimeter, see what else we can do, but you need to take her away. You're lucky I didn't shoot her."

John looked up at the sheriff who was now hovering above them. "Thank you, sir. I'm so sorry. She just hasn't been herself lately."

Sheriff Anderson shook his head, "If you want us to keep looking for your son then you need to get her the hell out of here. I can't trust her around my men."

"Yes sir, we'll leave right away," John said as he stood up and helped Mary to her feet.

The deputies began to pack up with a speed that bordered on eagerness, their relief at leaving the site was noticeable through their hurried movements. They moved with purpose, avoiding lingering near the shaft, their quick glances and hushed tones adding to the eerie feel of the morning.

Sheriff Anderson lingered at the doorway, his hat in hand, the lines on his face deepening as he prepared to share more unsettling news. He glanced back at John and Mary, who stood anxiously awaiting any information that might help make sense of the chaos enveloping their lives.

"Look, there's something else you should know," Sheriff Anderson began, his voice low and weighted with concern. "It's not just your son Ben we're worried about. There's a pattern here that's hard to ignore."

John's brow furrowed; his interest piqued. "What kind of pattern?"

The sheriff sighed, his gaze shifting between John and Mary. "Barbara's daughter, Joann, and Tony's kid, they've been missing for a while now. Tony likes to tell everyone she went to live with her mother in the next county over, but the truth is, she never made it. Both girls were last seen around these parts, and nobody's heard anything since."

Mary covered her mouth with her hand, her eyes wide with shock. "Both of them? You mean, they're missing just like Ben?"

"That's right," the sheriff nodded gravely. "And the troubling part is, all these disappearances happened right around here, near your new home. This land... it's got a history, and not a kind one. Some folks say it's cursed, that it swallows up anyone who gets too close. I don't usually buy into local superstitions, but I've been sheriff here long enough to know that sometimes, there's truth in old tales."

John leaned against the wall, feeling a chill despite the warmth of the day. "So, you think what's happening with Ben... it's connected to those girls?"

"It's possible," Sheriff Anderson admitted, his expression solemn. "This isn't the first time strange things have happened around these parts. We've had our fair share of oddities, and more often than not, they lead back to this area."

Mary felt a knot form in her stomach. "What can we do, Sheriff? How can we find our son?"

Sheriff Anderson met her gaze, his eyes sincere yet filled with regret. "We'll keep looking, of course. I've got my best men on it, and we're not giving up until we find Ben and the other kids. But you need to be careful, stay vigilant, and maybe consider staying somewhere else for a while."

John shook his head, his resolve firming. "We can't just leave, not if there's a chance Ben might come back. We have to stay, at least for now."

The sheriff nodded, understanding the father's determination. "I get it. Just make sure to lock your doors at night and keep a close eye on each other. Whatever's happening here, it's not ordinary, and it's not over."

With a final nod of assurance, Sheriff Anderson turned and walked down the porch steps, his figure receding into the twilight as John and Mary stood together, facing the looming uncertainty that now hung over their home like a dark cloud.

As the search team retreated through the forest, the silence returned, heavier than before. John and Mary were left standing by the gaping mouth of the mineshaft, the darkness below a silent testament to the mystery of their son's disappearance. The woods around them seemed to close in, the morning light dimming as if the forest itself was holding its breath, leaving them enveloped in an oppressive solitude.

BEN IS GONE

The morning wore on with a haunting quietude in Micaville. John and Mary mechanically packed a few essentials, their movements slow and methodical, as if trapped in a haze of grief. Emma hovered nearby, her eyes wide with confusion and sadness, mirroring the turmoil her parents tried to shield her from.

"Are we leaving, Mom?" Emma asked softly, her voice trembling.

Mary knelt down, forcing a faint smile. "Yes, sweetheart. We're going to stay somewhere else for a little while."

As the Harper family prepared to leave, Emma's voice cracked with emotion, breaking the heavy silence that had settled around them. "Why are we leaving?" she asked, her eyes wide and desperate. "Ben is still out there. How can we just leave him behind?"

John crouched down to her level, placing a gentle hand on her shoulder. His voice was steady, trying to instill a sense of calm in the midst of chaos. "Emma, we're not giving up on Ben, not ever," he assured her. "But staying here right now isn't helping. We need to clear our heads and come up with a better plan. Think of it as regrouping, so we can keep searching for him more effectively."

Emma nodded slowly, her gaze shifting between her parents, still struggling with the idea but trying to grasp the rationale her father presented.

Sheriff Anderson approached them once more, his footsteps soft on the ground. His expression was solemn as he offered a few words of reassurance. "John, Mary," he began gently, his voice imbued with empathy, "I'll keep my deputies on alert. If anything comes up or if you need anything at all, don't hesitate to call."

"Thank you, Sheriff," Mary responded, her voice barely above a whisper, grateful for the continued support.

As John turned the ignition key, the engine hummed to life, shattering the stifling silence that had enveloped them all. They were ready to leave, the oppressive air of Micaville pressing down as they sought distance from the haunting woods. But as the car began to roll forward, a soft, eerie melody sliced through the air, winding tightly around them, escalating rapidly in intensity.

Mary's body tensed, her eyes widening as she recognized the sound. It seemed to seep into the very fabric of the car, resonating with an urgent, unsettling tone that only Mary seemed to fully grasp.

In a sudden burst of frantic energy, Mary unbuckled her seatbelt and lunged at the car controls. Her hands, trembling yet driven by an unseen compulsion, ripped the keys from the ignition and flung them out the window into the dense underbrush beside the road.

John stared at her, the depth of their predicament dawning on him as he processed her words. The key's metallic clink as they vanished into the forest marked the end of their hopes for a quick escape, anchoring them to the haunted ground of their new home.

"Sweetheart! What are you doing?" John's voice was thick with confusion and rising alarm. He reached out to restrain her, his hands grappling with her arms as she struggled against him.

In the backseat, Emma pressed herself against the door, her eyes wide, tears streaming down her cheeks as she witnessed her mother's frenzied actions. "Mom, please, stop! Why are you doing this?"

But Mary was far from done. She shoved the door open and sprinted toward the front of the vehicle. Throwing herself onto the hood, she began clawing at the windshield wipers, tearing them away in a display of desperate strength.

John quickly exited the car and raced around to the front, his arms wrapping firmly around Mary, pulling her down from the hood. "We need to leave! This isn't safe!"

he shouted, trying to overcome the howling wind that mingled with the chilling melody.

Mary thrashed in his grip, her eyes darting around as if haunted by unseen forces. "We can't leave! It-it won't let us! We have to stay! It needs us!" Her voice broke, mirroring the eerie sounds that had invaded her mind.

"What the fuck! What are you doing?"John said, as he became more frustrated with Mary's actions.

"We can't leave! N-not yet," Mary's voice trembled, her eyes wild with fear and conviction. "It's safer if we...if we stay. Leaving now... it might make things worse."

THE NIGHTMARE CONTINUES

N ight enveloped the house, each shadow seeming to
whisper secrets in a language only fear could understand. Inside, the tension was palpable, a thick blanket
of unease that draped over every word and glance. John,
conflicted and weary, glanced out the window once more,
hoping to catch sight of anything that might offer them a
hint of what to do next.

That's when he saw them—two young girls in the yard,
their movements slow and eerie in the moonlight. They
were joined by a familiar figure: Ben. But there was something off about him; his usual vibrant demeanor was
nowhere to be seen. Instead, he stood limply between
thcm, as if controlled or deeply afraid.

Mary joined John at the window, her breath catching in her throat at the sight. "Babe, that's Ben with them. Go do something! Don't just fucking stand there. Go get our son."

The girls, holding hands with Ben, began to circle, their movements synchronized and deliberate. They began to chant in a haunting melody, their voices intertwining in a disturbing lullaby:

"Father gathers us tonight, under the moon's ghostly light, join us, join, don't fight, Father's joy, our plight."

Mary's hands flew to her mouth, stifling a sob. "H-he doesn't want to be with them. Look at him; something's for-forcing him to be there!"

John's face hardened, a mix of anger and fear etching his features. The sight of his son, manipulated and used in such a way, ignited a fury in him he hadn't felt before. Yet, alongside the anger was a piercing helplessness; the scene before him was beyond his understanding, beyond his control.

John's voice was a low murmur, battling the storm of conflict within. "We... we need to get him back," he said, but his tone wavered, betraying his inner turmoil. The part of him that was a father and a soldier screamed to charge into the darkness, to tear away whatever phantom hands held his son. Yet, another voice, insidious and chilling, whispered seductively in the recesses of his mind, urging him to leave Ben with the spectral girls, convincing him that perhaps that was where his son truly belonged.

Mary, her face streaked with tears, clutched at John's arm, her voice trembling with urgency. "How, babe? We can't just leave him with... with them. What can we do now?"

John's eyes were fixed on the haunting scene unfolding in their yard, his jaw clenched as he fought the dual urges battling within him. The girls' ghostly dance with Ben seemed almost ritualistic, a stark departure from the life of normalcy they once knew.

Finally, he spoke, his voice heavy with a resolve that felt more forced than felt. "I don't know, Mary. But acknowledging this nightmare is real—that's our starting point." He paused; the internal struggle clear in his eyes. "And then... we do whatever it takes to bring our son home."

But as they stood together, united in their fear and determination, John felt the malevolent voice grow louder, blaming Mary for their plight. It twisted his fear into anger, directing it at the woman who had stood by him through everything. Yet, somewhere deep down, the real John—the loving husband and father—fought to keep that darkness at bay.

Outside, the macabre dance continued, the eerie melody of the children's voices weaving a complex tapestry of dread and eerie promise over the Harper household. Each note seemed to tug at the fraying edges of John's sanity, a sinister lullaby for the chaos that had taken root in their lives.

John's resolve snapped like a dry twig underfoot. "Screw this," he growled, a raw edge of desperation in his voice. He stormed towards the door, his every motion fueled by a reckless urgency to end this nightmare. Mary's cries of caution faded behind him, drowned out by the thundering of his heartbeat.

He flung the door open, the cold night air slamming against him with an almost physical force. The world outside was suddenly, eerily silent—a stark contrast to the cacophony that had filled it moments ago. John moved his head left to right in search of anything moving across the yard. But there was nothing. No ghostly girls, no son caught in their chilling embrace. Just the empty turn of dusk and the whispering wind that seemed to mock his desperation. The night was falling fast and the dense forest was already engulfed in complete darkness.

"Ben!" John's voice tore through the silence, desperate and commanding. But only the echo of his own cry came back to him, bouncing off the trees that bordered their property. He stepped forward, the grass wet under his boots, his flashlight darting from one dark corner to another, searching for any sign of movement, any hint of where they might have gone.

Nothing. As if the earth had swallowed them whole.

Inside the house, Emma clung to the window, her small face pressed against the glass, eyes wide and filled with tears. She watched her father's figure moving frantically in the yard, a sense of dread tightening around her heart.

Mary appeared at the doorway, her face pale and drawn, her eyes wide with fear. "John?" she called out, her voice quivering. "Did you find him?"

He turned to her, the flashlight's beam trembling in his unsteady hand, and shook his head slowly. "They're gone. Just... gone. Like they were never here." His voice was hollow, the defeat and confusion palpable.

The silence hung between them, oppressive and thick. Emma's soft sobs could now be heard over the silence, adding a heartbreaking soundtrack to the scene. John felt a mix of relief and terror; relief that the haunting visage was gone, but terror at what this sudden disappearance might mean for Ben's safety.

Mary stepped closer; her fear mirrored in John's eyes. "What do we do now?" she whispered, her voice barely carrying over the stillness.

John's fist clenched at his side, his initial surge of action fading into helplessness. "I don't know, Mary. I don't know," he admitted, his gaze drifting back to the ominously quiet woods. The night seemed to close in around them, the darkness not just a lack of light, but a tangible presence that weighed on their spirits.

Together, they stood at the threshold, the cold breeze nipping at their skin, the uncertainty of their next steps looming as large as the darkness that had claimed their son. The peace of the night was a cruel irony to the storm raging in their hearts.

"Ben!" John called out again, his voice echoing into the silence. "Ben, where are you?"

There was no answer. It was as if they simply disappeared.

"We have to find him," Mary said, her voice tinged with desperation. "We can't lose him. I just know he's out there."

John nodded; his jaw set with determination. "We'll search every inch of this place if we have to. If he's out here we'll find him."

"Okay," Mary's voice quivered, "Emma and I are coming with you. We can't—can't separate. I'm just... too scared to be apart."

"I agree, sweets. Let's all head out there together."

John, Mary, and Emma ventured back into the woods, their flashlights slicing through the darkness as they moved. The haunting melody of the whistling wrapped around them like a chilling embrace. Alongside it, John wrestled with an insidious voice that infiltrated his thoughts, urging him to deny the eerie events unfolding before them.

"Nothing is wrong. It's all in your head," the voice whispered, tempting John with the comfort of denial. But he couldn't succumb, not with the stakes so high.

"Screw this," John muttered, his voice filled with a mix of defiance and fear. "This is real. He's my son, and I'm bringing him back."

Mary and Emma walked close behind him; their expressions fraught with worry. They could hear John's muttered declarations, his tone one of a man arguing with an unseen adversary. His words were punctuated by pauses, as if he were listening to responses they couldn't hear. This invisible dialogue sent shivers down Mary's spine, and she exchanged a frightened glance with Emma.

"Babe, who are you talking to?" Mary asked, her voice trembling.

"It's nothing, just trying to keep my head straight," John replied, almost too quickly, his voice a brittle mask over his inner turmoil. His denial did little to ease the tension, his ongoing murmurs feeding the ominous atmosphere.

Emma clutched Mary's hand tighter, her eyes wide and frightened as she watched her father. "Mom, what's happening to Dad?" she whispered, her voice barely audible over the rustle of the undergrowth.

"He's just stressed, honey," Mary assured her daughter, though her faith in that explanation was faltering. She kept her gaze fixed on John, observing the way his flashlight beam shook slightly as they moved deeper into the forest.

John's internal battle was palpable, the struggle between acknowledging the supernatural forces at play and clinging to rational explanations. "I'm not imagining this," he continued, half under his breath as if to convince himself as much as the voices in his head. "We all saw the two girls, didn't we? This isn't just me."

The path before them seemed to stretch endlessly, the darkness intensifying around each bend. The whistling grew louder, more defined, as if drawing them further into its web. With every step, the psychological strain on John mounted, his sporadic admissions of fear and snippets of argument with himself painting a portrait of a man teetering on the brink of despair.

Mary and Emma followed closely, their concern growing with each disjointed utterance from John. The night enveloped them completely now, the only sounds were their heavy breathing and the distant, eerie melody that seemed to call them deeper into the woods.

From somewhere in the darkness, a voice emerged—clear, distinct, and hauntingly familiar. "I'm over here, come play with us. You don't need to be afraid anymore." The words floated through the thick foliage, tinged with a cheerful menace that seemed out of place in the quiet forest.

Emma's grip on Mary's hand became firmer, her pulse quickening as she processed the voice that sounded so much like her brother. "Mom, Dad," she whispered, her voice trembling with a mix of hope and fear. "That's Ben, isn't it? Why does he sound like that?"

Mary's face went pale, her eyes searching the shadowy spaces between the trees as she nodded. "It must be him," she responded, trying to keep her voice steady for Emma's sake, though her heart raced with a cocktail of emotions.

John stood still, listening intently. The voice came again, mingled this time with laughter- Ben's laughter-echoing through the trees in a way that was both comforting and chilling. "Ben!" John called out, his voice echoing through the woods. "We're coming, buddy! Stay where you are!"

The laughter and voice seemed to play with them, coming from multiple directions, elusive and ethereal, dancing just beyond their reach. It beckoned them deeper into the forest, leading them on a path that felt increasingly uncertain.

Mary led the way, her steps hurried and purposeful despite the gnawing unease that clawed at her insides. "We have to find him," she said under her breath, pulling Emma through the underbrush, over fallen logs, each step drawing them deeper into the heart of the woods.

The canopy above thickened, casting dappled shadows across their path, the fading light creating illusions that seemed to shift and move with a life of their own. The whispers of Ben's voice continued a siren call that was impossible to ignore, drawing them forward.

As they moved, the air around them seemed to grow colder, the atmosphere charged with an intangible tension. Every snapped twig underfoot, every rustle of leaves felt like a whisper from the woods, urging them onward, deeper into the darkness that held secrets just out of sight.

John, Mary, and Emma moved as one, driven by a desperate hope to find Ben, clinging to the sound of his voice in the darkness, each call weaving a complex tapestry of dread and determination as they navigated the uncertain terrain of the haunted woods.

As they ventured further, the laughter grew louder, filling the air with a bittersweet melody that tugged at their hearts. Emma's eyes darted nervously between the shifting shadows, her fingers tightening around Mary's hand as they navigated the maze of trees and tangled undergrowth.

"Ben, please," John called out again, his voice a desperate plea in the gathering twilight. "Come to us, son. We're here."

"We have to keep going," Mary urged, her voice trembling with emotion. "He's close. I can feel it."

And then, as suddenly as it had begun, the laughter faded into an eerie silence. The air grew still.

John halted, his senses on high alert as he scanned their surroundings. "Where did it go?" he murmured; his voice tinged with frustration.

Mary's gaze swept the clearing ahead, her heart sinking with a mix of disappointment and lingering hope. "I don't know," she whispered, her voice barely audible over the rustling leaves. "But we can't give up. We have to keep searching."

As they turned to retrace their steps, the forest seemed to sigh, a mournful lament that echoed their sense of loss and longing. They walked in silence, each lost in their thoughts and prayers for a miracle that seemed just out of reach.

As they finally emerged from the thick woods, night had fallen completely, enveloping them in a darkness so profound it seemed even the moon dared not shine. A flicker of hope still burned within them, fueled by the lingering echoes of Ben's laughter that seemed to drift through the trees—a spectral reminder of what they were fighting for. Exhausted from the afternoon's relentless search, both physically and mentally, they trudged forward, clinging to the belief that somewhere in the dense, whispering darkness, their son was still waiting to be found.

The search for Ben had yielded no answers, only a deepening sense of dread and an increasing realization that the woods held secrets that defied comprehension. The laughter had faded with the darkness of the forest, but the feeling of being watched and the sense of impending doom remained.

They returned to the house, their hearts heavy with the weight of their failure and the growing fear of what lay ahead. The woods behind them were silent now, but the echoes of their search would haunt them long after the daylight had faded.

The day passed in a blur of exhaustion and bleakness. The woods had become a place of nightmares, a dark and nasty presence that seemed to mock their every attempt to find their lost child.

As midnight approached, the stillness outside grew thick and heavy, as if the night itself was holding its breath, complicit in the terrors afflicting the Harper family. Inside the dimly lit living room, John, Mary, and Emma sat tightly together, a lone lamp casting their long shadows against the walls that seemed almost to breathe in the quiet. The air hung dense with unease, each groan of the old house underscoring their profound isolation.

Mary's eyes were wide, her face pale and drawn as she clutched John's hand with a desperate strength. John's brow was furrowed, his jaw set tightly as he tried to mask his own fear, to be the anchor his family needed even as his heart raced uncontrollably. Emma, nestled between them, tried to appear brave, but her occasional shivers betrayed her terror.

The silence was a living thing, heavy and expectant, as if waiting for the family's resolve to crack. Each passing moment felt like an eternity, the tension building to an almost unbearable level. They were trapped in a chilling narrative, the dark woods surrounding their home like a malevolent barrier, cutting them off from the world they once knew.

In this grim tableau, the Harper family found themselves grappling not just with the fear of what lurked outside, but with the growing terror within their minds. As the clock ticked towards midnight, the boundary between reality and nightmare thinned, leaving them caught in the grip of an unfolding horror that promised no easy escape.

THE SHADOW WITHIN

As they settled in, a subdued gloom crept through the windows of the house, casting long, dark voids across the room where the family gathered. The day had been long and arduous, spent searching for Ben deep in the woods, each passing hour bringing them no closer to finding him. As they regrouped at home, the exhaustion of their fruitless efforts hung heavily in the air.

A floor lamp in the corner of the kitchen was the sole source of light, its soft glow casting shifting patterns on the walls and floor. The subtle movements of light lent a transient, flickering quality to the room, mirroring the flicker of hope that had waned with the setting sun.

Mary sat at the table, staring blankly at the untouched plates of dinner before her. The food was cold now, the steam that had once risen from the hearty meal settling into a chill that seemed to seep into the bones of the house. Now and then, she'd lift her eyes to the dim outline of the window, watching and waiting for something to happen. Holding out hope that Ben would miraculously appear at the door.

Emma, wrapped in a blanket, was seated on a chair next to Mary. Her face was drawn, the shadows under her eyes marking the day's toll. The room was quiet, save for the occasional shifting in their seats and the rhythmic ticking of the clock on the wall. The usual comfort found in their evening routines was absent, replaced by a palpable tension.

The silence was not peaceful but charged, filled with the echoes of the day's desperate calls and the haunting absence of Ben's voice in response. As the crescent moon lifted higher into the sky, the reality of their situation seemed to solidify—their home, a supposed haven, now felt like a holding space for their worries and the uncertainty of the night to come.

John finally stopped his restless movements and turned to look at his family, his expression a mixture of determination and fatigue. "We'll keep looking," he said, his voice low but resolute. "As soon as it's light again, we go back out."

Mary nodded silently, her gaze returning to the window, where the boundary between sky and land blurred into pitch black. The night ahead loomed, promising another stretch of restless vigilance.

Mary reached across the table, her fingers cold and trembling. The dim glow from the lamp cast stark lines of worry on her face. "Babe, what the hell do we do now? We've screamed ourselves raw in those damn woods, and there's nothing. Where else can we even look?" Her voice was raw with fatigue, edged with a desperate frustration.

John met her gaze his face showing signs of defeat, but his words promising results. "We've got to figure out what's going on here. It's not just trees and shadows out there—it's like the whole damn forest is against us, hiding Ben." His voice carried a weary strength, trying to infuse some sense of control over the chaos.

Tears welled up in Mary's eyes, spilling over as her despair deepened. "But how? We've turned every leaf, we've broken our backs out there. What are we missing?"

John turned his head, staring out the window where the dark shapes of the trees loomed ominously against the night sky. "There's got to be something we haven't seen, some fucking clue we've overlooked. There has to be," he muttered, half to himself, as if trying to piece together a puzzle in his mind.

"We're chasing ghosts," Mary choked out, her voice a whisper of defeat. "It feels like we're just chasing shadows, going round in circles."

As the clock ticked closer to midnight, John's resolve began to fracture under the strain. Abruptly, his grip on Mary's hand tightened to the point of pain. "Why don't you just have another one of your goddamn premonitions, Mary?" he snapped, the harshness in his voice slicing through the heavy silence of the room.

The venom in his words shocked them both. Emma flinched; her eyes wide with fear. Mary recoiled, hurt and confusion written across her face. "Babe, what's happening to you?"

John paced the room, his movements erratic. He muttered under his breath, a disturbing dialogue with himself. "No, not now. I don't want to say these things. Get out of my head," he hissed, clenching his fists.

The room fell silent but for the soft crackle of the lamp. Mary's voice was gentle, laden with worry. "John, you're scaring me. You're scaring Emma. What voices are you talking about?"

Breaking down, John's façade crumbled, revealing a man tormented by unseen forces. "Mary, there's something inside me... it pushes me to say things, to push you away. I don't know how to stop it," he confessed, his voice breaking.

The vulnerability in his confession struck a chord with Mary. Her earlier hurt shifted into concern. "We're here for you, babe. We'll get through this together," she assured him, reaching out to bring him back into an embrace.

Their conversation lingered in the charged silence of the kitchen, filled with a mix of fear, resolve, and a raw shred of hope. Outside, the quiet woods stood watch, an inscrutable and vast presence that seemed to await their next move. The night stretched ahead, laden with the weight of their unresolved anguish, as they braced themselves to face another day in their relentless quest.

As if in answer to John's unspoken thoughts, the house was suddenly filled with a faint, rhythmic tapping sound. It was coming from the front door, a slow, deliberate knock that seemed out of place in the oppressive silence.

John and Mary exchanged a puzzled look, their hearts racing. John stood and approached the door, his steps hesitant and wary. He peered through the peephole but saw nothing.

"Who is it?" he called out; his voice noticeably shaken.

As the tapping persisted, growing more insistent, John and Mary exchanged a look of tense apprehension. Mary stood close behind John, who reached cautiously for the door handle. His fingers trembled slightly as he turned it, the metallic click sounding unnaturally loud in the silent house.

The door creaked open, revealing an empty porch bathed in a dim, eerie light. A faint mist swirled around the edges of the doorframe, carrying with it the sharp, clean scent of pine. The cold air that rushed in seemed to push against them, as if warning them back.

"Hello?" John's voice echoed slightly, his tone hopeful yet wary. There was no reply, only the soft whisper of the wind rustling through the trees.

Stepping outside, John raised his flashlight, its beam slicing through the fog. The light of the moon struggled to pierce the dense mist that hugged the ground, creating shadows that seemed to shift and move with a life of their own. As he scanned the yard, his light caught a startling sight near the tree line: three figures stood ominously—two young girls and a smaller figure that looked hauntingly like Ben.

"Mary!" John yelled. "They're back. The girls are back, and Ben is with them again."

For a moment, they just stood there, the figures eerily still. Then, as if noticing John's gaze, the childlike figure waved and smiled—a gesture so unsettlingly out of place that it sent a shiver down John's spine. Before he could react or call out, the figures turned and vanished into the woods with unnerving speed.

"Nothing here," John muttered, more to reassure himself as he retreated to the safety of the doorway. "I'm going crazy... were all going mad," he said half-heartedly, not believing his own words.

Mary nodded, her eyes wide with a mix of fear and confusion. "Did you see them?" she whispered; her voice tight with anxiety.

John didn't answer as he shut the door firmly behind them, locking it with a decisive clack. The sound of the bolt sliding into place was supposed to offer reassurance, but as they stood in the dimly lit hallway, the isolation of their home felt more like a trap than a sanctuary.

The tapping intensified, evolving from a disturbing irregularity into a relentless, harrowing beat. It began at the living room window—a series of sharp, purposeful knocks that shattered the night's silence. Then, with eerie precision, the sound migrated, tracing the outline of the house as if some unseen predators were methodically circling its prey. Clutching Emma tightly, Mary wrapped her arms protectively around her daughter, shielding her from the unseen menace lurking just beyond the glass.

John, his heart pounding, approached the living room window with his flashlight in hand. As he shone the light through the glass, the tapping intensified, now loud and forceful, as if demanding attention. Pressing his face closer to the cold glass, John's breath fogged the surface momentarily before he saw it—two pale hands sliding slowly down the outside of the pane.

The sight jolted him, but it was the whispering voice that froze his blood: "We need to eat, John... we need to eat." The words slithered through the cracks of the window frame, malevolent and chilling.

John recoiled, horror surging through him as he stumbled back. "Get the fuck away! We have nothing for you. Leave us alone!" he shouted, his voice rough with fear and anger.

But the voice persisted, unyielding and eerie. "But Ben is so hungry."

The implications of those words twisted in John's gut, terror mixing with a fierce protectiveness. He raced to check the locks on all the doors and windows, Mary following close behind, her face pale and her eyes wide with fear. They moved together, securing each entry point, the silence of the house now a mocking reminder of their vulnerability.

As they worked, the tapping followed, a constant reminder of the presence lurking just outside. When they reached the back door, Mary gasped. Through the frosted glass, they could see shadows moving, swaying in the dim light of dawn that was struggling to break through the heavy fog.

"What do they want?" Mary's voice was barely a whisper, choked with fear.

Before John could answer, a soft, sinister laugh echoed against the glass, and the voice came again, this time a sing-song mockery: "Won't you feed us, John? It's been so long since we've eaten."

John grabbed a kitchen chair, propping it under the doorknob as an extra measure. He turned to Mary; his expression set with grim resolve. "We need to stay away from the windows, barricade ourselves in until daylight fully comes. Maybe they'll leave with the light."

In a tense moment of instinct, John snatched a kitchen knife from the drawer, his mind racing for a more formidable weapon. He wished for a firearm, something with weight and immediacy, but Mary's steadfast opposition to guns in the house, a condition set when he returned from military service, left them unarmed in a way that felt suddenly precarious. John's fingers tightened around the knife's handle; his gaze fixed on the shadows flitting across the windows.

The urge to confront whatever—or whoever—was outside surged within him, yet the invasive whispers in his mind sapped his resolve, urging him to stay indoors, to hide rather than fight. The chilling reality of his helplessness gnawed at him as he backed away from the window, pulling Mary and Emma closer.

They hastily pushed a kitchen table against the door, fashioning a makeshift barricade. The taps persisted, now underscored by whispers and the eerie echo of laughter that seemed to encircle the house with an ominous, invisible presence. Each shadow that danced at the edge of their vision, each flicker of the light, felt like a direct response from the house to the sinister spectacle unfolding outside.

As they huddled together, waiting for the dawn to strengthen and drive away the night's horrors, Mary and John clung to each other, the reality of their situation settling around them like a cold shroud. Whatever was outside was not just after Ben—it was after them all, and the light of day seemed a lifetime away.

Ben's voice continued to echo hauntingly through the night air, a desperate plea woven with unsettling hunger.

"Mom, Dad, I'm so hungry. Why are you doing this? Why don't you want to play with me?" His words felt like a physical blow to Mary, each syllable soaked in despair and manipulation, pulling at her heartstrings with unbearable force.

As Mary's resolve weakened, and her hands reached shakily for the door lock, a horrifying scream pierced the night, followed by the sickening sound of something wet and heavy striking the window. A crimson spray of blood splattered across the glass, casting grotesque patterns in the dim light provided by the porch lantern. From outside, Ben's voice shifted to a shrill, panicked tone, "Help me, Mom! They're going to kill me!"

The terror in his voice was deep, and it nearly broke Mary completely. Tears streaming down her face, she frantically fumbled with the lock, her maternal instincts overwhelming her senses. "I have to help him, John! I can't let them hurt our boy!"

John, his own heart racing with fear and confusion, grasped her firmly by the shoulders and pulled her away from the door with all the strength he could muster. "Mary, stop! That's not Ben—not our Ben," he shouted over her sobs, his voice raw with desperation. "Whatever is out there, it's using him against us. We can't fall for it!"

Mary struggled against his grip, her eyes wild with fear and desperation. "But what if it is him? What if he needs us?" Her voice cracked under the strain of her emotions, torn between the instinct to protect her child and the chilling evidence that something far more sinister was at play.

John held her tightly. "Listen to me, sweetheart. We need to stay inside. We need to protect ourselves and Emma. We can't help Ben if we're caught in whatever trap they've set for us."

THE BLOOD

The blood on the window glistened ominously as the voice outside began to fade, replaced by a low, menacing laugh that chilled them to the bone. It was clear that the eerie children beyond their walls were toying with them, feeding on their fear.

Inside, the house felt like a besieged fortress, the horrors of the outside world clawing at their sanctuary, trying to draw them out. John, Mary, and Emma sank to the floor by the door, holding each other, their minds racing for a solution, their hearts heavy with the haunting possibility that their son was lost to a darkness they could neither understand nor combat.

As they returned to the kitchen, Emma's soft, frightened voice interrupted their thoughts. "Mommy, Daddy... I heard something."

John and Mary turned to her, their hearts skipping a beat. "What did you hear, sweetie?" John asked gently.

Emma hugged her stuffed bear she had been clinging to, "I heard... whispers. They were saying something about the house."

John and Mary exchanged another worried look. "What were the whispers saying?" Mary pressed.

Emma's small face was pale, her eyes wide with fear. "They said the house... the house is watching us... watching me."

John shook his head, finding it impossible to believe what was happening to them. The house had never felt like a safe haven, or a place where they could escape the horrors of the outside world. But now, it seemed as if the very walls of their home had become a prison of their own making.

John looked over at Mary and Emma who were holding onto one another as if they were listening to see if someone was in the house. "I'm going to take a look around and make sure nobody broke in."

"Daddy, please don't leave us."

John gave Emma a reassuring look, the tension evident in his eyes. "Don't worry, sweetheart, I'll be right back," he promised, his voice steady despite the chaos around them. He glanced at both Mary and Emma, adding, "Try to stay calm while I'm gone." Deep down, John knew that after everything that had happened, the likelihood of any of them finding rest was next to none. The house felt too charged with fear, every sound magnifying their anxiety.

John rose from the couch, feeling as if the dense air of the room clung to him, hindering his every step. With one hand gripping his flashlight and the other on the long kitchen knife, its cold metal a meager comfort against the unease that permeated the house. As he moved towards Ben's room, his footsteps on the carpet were the only sound, a soft shuffle that seemed unnaturally loud in the thick silence.

He reached Ben's room, and the door creaked ominously on its hinges as he pushed it open. The flashlight's beam revealed a scene of disarray: drawers were pulled open, their contents strewn about, and toys and clothes conspicuously absent. The chaos struck a deep chord of dread within him, the once familiar space transformed into a tableau of turmoil.

John's journey through the house was a tightrope walk between reality and the creeping sense of something amiss. Each room told the same story of intrusion, the light from his flashlight casting grotesque forms that seemed to twitch at the edge of his vision, as though mocking his efforts to find normalcy.

Descending into the basement, the change in temperature was immediate and chilling. The overhead bulb flickered reluctantly to life, throwing harsh shadows against the bare concrete, elongating them into dark, menacing figures. A faint, unsettling noise broke the usual silence—a rustling that seemed to emanate from beneath the floorboards. It was too deliberate to be dismissed as mere house noises.

"Ben, is that you?" John called into the oppressive darkness. His voice echoed back at him, distorted and hollow. A brief silence followed, and then a soft, muffled cry cut through the stillness, nearly sending his heart through his chest. It sounded like a plea, a desperate, stifled sob.

Frantically, John searched the floor for any sign of a hidden entrance, his hands sweeping over the cold, rough surface, finding nothing but the immovable solidity of wooden planks and dust. Doubt gnawed at him, the sound of that cry embedding itself in his mind, real or imagined—a cruel trick or a genuine plea for help?

Am I losing it like my damn wife? Hearing things? He muttered to himself, a mix of fear and frustration in his voice.

Reluctantly, he turned off the light and ascended back to the ground floor, the echo of that desperate sound following him.

As John sank into the dimly lit living room, his silhouette was a stark contrast against the faint glow from the lamps. The fear etched on his face was palpable, casting a chill that matched the draft whispering through the room. He gathered his thoughts, his voice a low rumble in the quiet, as he started to unravel the disturbing events he'd encountered throughout the house.

"The house, it's been turned inside out," John began, his tone reflecting the severity of the intrusion. "Every room

has been gone through. Drawers pulled open, our shit sc
attered... It's like something was desperately searching for
something specific, or someone was sending us a message."

He paused, swallowing hard, the memory of the disarray
vivid in his mind. "I don't think it's random though—the
focus was clear. Ben's room took the worst of it. His
clothes, some toys... gone. It's as if whatever did this knew
exactly what would piss us off the most."

The room absorbed his words, the shadows seeming to
lean closer, drawn by the tale of disturbance. John's voice
became even more hushed as he recounted the chilling
experience in the basement. "And there's something else,
something crazy happened down there, I heard noises,
like something moving beneath the floorboards. I called
out, half out of hope, half out of dread. And something...
something cried back. It sounded like a muffled cry from
below us."

Emma clutched the blanket tighter around her, her eyes
reflecting the lamp's flicker, her mind racing with the implications. The thought of an unseen presence lurking
right beneath them was more horrifying than any ghost
story she'd ever heard.

John looked from Emma to Mary, his eyes grave. "This
isn't just a break-in or a prank. It's as if we're being manipulated, toyed with by something that understands exactly
how to frighten us. The way it's using Ben's belongings...
it's personal and calculated."

The silence that followed was thick, almost suffocating, as the words hung heavily in the air.

"We need to stick together," John concluded, his voice barely above a whisper, yet carrying a determined edge. "Whatever is happening, it decided to fuck with us for some reason, our house and I don't know why. We're in this together though, and we need to stand strong."

John's eyes flashed with wild, desperate energy as he suddenly stood, his entire body tensing. He thrust his arms out to his sides, his fists clenched tightly. "Do you hear that? We are not afraid of you!" he bellowed, his voice echoing through the house, cracking with strain. "Give us our son back and leave us the hell alone!"

As the words tore from his throat, John's mind wrestled with the menacing whispers that clawed at the edges of his consciousness, urging him to doubt, to fear, to surrender. But at this moment, fueled by a mix of fear and defiance, he tried to reclaim control, to push back against the unseen forces that seemed intent on tearing his family apart. Mary and Emma stared at him, their eyes wide not just with fear of the haunting but with alarm at John's unraveling state.

John's breaths came heavy and ragged as he lowered his arms, the silence swelling around them once again. "We won't let them win," he muttered more to himself than to Mary or Emma, as if trying to convince his own besieged mind just as much as reassure his family.

They drew closer on the couch, their proximity a small comfort against the growing dread. Outside, the wind howled louder, as if angry, the night enveloping the house in an impenetrable darkness that seemed eager to swallow them whole. The idea of something beneath them, possibly listening, possibly waiting, turned every shadow into a potential hiding place, every noise a potential signal. As they sat together, the reality of their situation wrapped around them like a cold mist, unrelenting and unfathomable.

Mary's eyes, red-rimmed and wide, met his as she stood up, her body tense. "Babe, you heard him! That was Ben's voice, I just know it." Her voice broke, a mix of desperation and a raw, guttural fear. "But why his things? Why only his? He's still out there."

John finally broke the silence, his decision heavy with an unspoken resignation. "We stay put for now. We keep everything locked down and wait for daylight. It's all we can do." His voice was low, the words almost a defeat.

Mary nodded, collapsing back into her chair, her eyes fixed on the windows where the last light flickered against the glass. "We need to keep everything locked, every door, every window," she murmured, her voice hollow.

They moved through the house once again, checking each lock, the metallic clicks a cold soundtrack to their grim task. John pulled the curtains shut, blocking out the creeping twilight, while Emma and Mary turned on a few more lamps, the light weak but comforting against the encroaching gloom.

It's So Dark and Cold

The night stretched on, each hour a test of their sanity. Jumping at every sound, flinching at the wind's eerie moans, they sat together, a family united by fear, waiting for a dawn that seemed an eternity away.

Mary huddled with Emma on the worn sofa, her arms wrapped protectively around her daughter. Her whispers mixed with the deeper shadows, her words a stream of disjointed murmurs that filled the room with an unsettling undercurrent.

"I-it's so dark, Mommy..." Emma stuttered, her voice quivering with fear. "Ben says it's... it's too dark..."

John paced the room relentlessly, each step echoing against the wood floors, amplifying his deep-rooted fear.

The house seemed to pulse with a life of its own, the walls whispering secrets in a language only madness could understand.

Suddenly, the room grew colder, a tangible presence filling the space that made Mary clutch Emma closer. John stopped pacing and listened; a burst of soft, sinister laughter fluttered through the air, not just in their ears but as if echoing inside their minds.

"We can't just sit here. These whispers—Emma's hearing them clearer now. We have to do something," Mary's voice was a low murmur, nearly drowned out by the growing chorus of whispers.

John looked up, his face pale. "I know, Mary, but what can we do? Screw it. I'm going out there. I'm going to find these assholes who broke in."

From the hallway, a sudden crash jolted them into heightened alertness. It wasn't just a noise; it was an intrusion, a violent shattering of the fragile barrier they had hoped would protect them from the house's darker influences.

"Did you hear that?" John's voice was sharp, a spike of adrenaline cutting through the thicker dread.

Mary nodded, terror taking root. "Ben! Is that you?"

John stood in front of Mary and Emma, his soldier instincts kicking in, "something else is here with us."

Without waiting, John moved toward the sound, his footsteps heavy and determined. Mary and Emma stayed back, clinging to each other as the air filled with a palpable tension.

John reached the hallway and flicked his flashlight beam across the darkened corridor, the light trembling in his unsteady grip. The source of the noise became horrifyingly apparent: an upturned chair lay several feet away from the kitchen table, as if thrown by unseen hands. The sudden and unexplainable movement of the chair in the otherwise still house was like a scream in the silence—an abrupt and terrifying declaration of presence.

"Nothing here..." he called back, his voice filled with a tension that did little to reassure. "Just the chair... it's like it was thrown across the room."

Returning to the living room, John's silhouette was a dark shape against the single bulb that shined from above. The shadows seemed to cling to him, as if reluctant to let go. Emma shivered, whispering into Mary's ear, "He says we can't leave, Mommy. The house won't let us. He said that it's nearly time to join him."

Mary's eyes blazed with a fiery resolve as she stood up, her voice cutting through the tense atmosphere. "I'm not going to say it again, babe. We can't just sit around here. We're not doing anything."

John tried to assert some control, his voice firm. "We'll leave at first light. We'll pack what we can and get far, far away from here."

But Mary's anger flared as she cut him off. "We are not going anywhere! Ben is still out there, and I'm not leaving until we find him. Whatever took him, took his stuff for a reason. They have him somewhere!" Her voice was sharp, each word laden with urgency and fear. "Why don't you man the fuck up and go get our son back?"

The tension between Mary and John reached a boiling point as Mary's insistence met John's stubborn resistance. "We're going together," Mary declared, her voice sharp and unyielding.

"The hell you will," John retorted, his frustration peaking. "Alright, you two stay here while I go get chopped up into a million pieces by some psychotic locals."

Mary's face hardened, her words laced with a cold, biting sarcasm. "Well, I hope you find Ben before they find you."

John's anger flared at her remark, his voice rising in disbelief. "You're fucking sick."

The escalating argument was abruptly cut off by Emma's scream. The piercing sound filled the room, silencing both John and Mary. Tears streamed down her face as she stood up, her body trembling with a mix of fear and anger. "Fuck... fuck...fuck. Can you two just fucking stop?" she yelled, her voice cracking under the strain. "My baby brother is out there, and you guys are in here fighting like this is some kind of sick game!"

The raw emotion in Emma's voice struck John and Mary deeply, the reality of their situation crashing back down on them. The room fell into a stunned silence, the weight of Emma's words hanging heavily in the air. They looked at each other, the heat of their anger dissolving into a shared pain, each feeling the sting of their daughter's words.

John and Mary slowly approached Emma; their movements hesitant but purposeful. John reached out first, placing a hand on her shoulder, his voice soft and remorseful. "You're right, Emma. I'm sorry. We shouldn't be fighting—not now."

Mary nodded in agreement; her voice equally subdued. "She's right, John. We need to be in this together, for Ben. For all of us."

As they gathered their things to retreat to a safer part of the house for the remainder of the night, the whispers intensified, growing clearer and more urgent. No longer mere echoes of some haunted past, they now resonated like stark warnings, or darker still, as direct threats. The air around them thickened with tension, each word weaving a heavier sense of foreboding into the night.

"Find the secrets..." the voices hissed around them, chillingly clear. "Or be taken... one by one."

The family's tense silence deepened as the night grew heavier, the interior lights casting a stark contrast against the pitch-black outside. Every sound was magnified, the stillness of the night making the atmosphere inside even more stifling.

Suddenly, a faint scratching noise echoed from the kitchen, slicing through the quiet. John's instincts kicked in; he stood abruptly, his movements quick and sharp as he made his way to the kitchen. The floorboards creaked under his hurried steps; the sound eerie in the tense silence. His hand found the cold handle of the knife he had left on the counter, gripping it tightly as his eyes scanned the dimly lit room.

As he turned to head back, a loud smash against the living room window jolted him. He rushed back, only to see the gruesome sight of an owl's bloodied carcass sliding down the glass, leaving a streak of crimson in its wake. The sudden, violent act against the window pane sent a shock of fear through them all.

As John returned to where Mary and Emma were waiting, his steps hesitant, his face shadowed in the dim light, the voices in his head grew louder, more insistent. "It's just an owl," he said quickly, trying to calm his nerves as much as theirs. "Must've hit the window by accident."

Mary's patience snapped, her voice rising in frustration. "John, this isn't about local kids or accidents! Don't you see what's happening?" she implored, desperation threading through her words.

John began to pace, the internal voices twisting his thoughts. They whispered venomously, blaming Mary for their plight. "She brought this upon us... invited them into our home, into our lives," he muttered, almost believing the dark chorus in his mind.

His words grew erratic, a stream of consciousness that veered between blame and confusion. "Is it Mary? Is it all of us losing our minds?" he rambled, his voice tinged with hysteria.

Suddenly, he stopped, his expression changing as he looked back at Mary and Emma. His features softened momentarily as clarity seemed to fight through the fog of manipulation. "I'm sorry," he said, his voice cracking with sincerity. "These voices... they're telling me it's all because of you, that you invited this darkness. But I know that's not true." His apology was heartfelt, yet his eyes betrayed the ongoing struggle within, caught between the real and the insidious suggestions of unseen forces.

Mary and Emma exchanged a glance, the event adding another layer of dread to the night. "We should move to the back room," Mary suggested, her voice trembling. "There are fewer windows there. It might be safer, or at least feel that way."

John nodded in agreement, the knife still in hand as a meager sense of security. They gathered the few things they could carry quickly—flashlights, and blankets, and moved to a smaller room at the back of the house. This room felt more contained, the walls closer together providing a semblance of safety from whatever lurked beyond their home.

As they settled into the cramped space, the close walls seemed to offer a buffer from the vast and unknown terrors outside. The minimal windows were a relief, reducing the haunting visuals of what might be waiting in the darkness. They positioned themselves away from the glass, huddled together, listening to the wind howl around the corners of the house, each gust a reminder of their fragile barrier between the known and the unknown.

POOL OF BLOOD

As they sat tightly together, a new, chilling sound broke the silence: a soft, rhythmic dripping that echoed through the stillness. Mary, her nerves already frayed, tilted her head, straining to identify the source. Her eyes widened with horror as she noticed a dark stain slowly spreading across the ceiling above them, the droplets growing heavier, falling faster, until it became clear—it was b lood.

The blood dripped steadily, forming a small, dark pool on the wooden floor below. The sight was chilling, and the room felt colder, as if the very air was thickening with dread.

Emma, pale and visibly shaking, clutched her mother's arm. "Mommy, it wants me," she whispered, her voice quivering with fear. "The voice, it's saying it wants me..."

John's face turned ashen. "No one is taking you anywhere," he said firmly, though his voice betrayed his terror.

Mary looked between Emma and John, her heart pounding uncontrollably. "Let's just get the hell out of here, just leave this place," she pleaded, her voice breaking.

But as she spoke, the whispering climaxed into a clear, menacing voice that filled the room. "Give us the girl, and you are free to go," it boomed, resonating with a malice that seemed to seep into their very bones.

The demand was too much for Mary. Her vision blurred, her breaths short and ragged, and she felt the room spin wildly around her. Overwhelmed by fear and desperation, she fainted, collapsing onto the couch as darkness swallowed her consciousness.

Mary awoke with a start, gasping for air as she clawed her way out of a horrifying nightmare. The room was bathed in the soft glow of a single lamp on the coffee table, casting long, eerie shadows against the walls that seemed to dance in the corner of her eye. She blinked rapidly, her heart racing, as she tried to distinguish between the remnants of her dream and the oppressive reality of the house.

She sat up, disoriented, her heart racing as she scanned the room. John was slumped against the armchair, his features relaxed in sleep. Emma lay curled up beside her on the couch, her breathing even and steady. However, the emptiness of Ben's absence hung heavy in the air—his laughter, his energy, all painfully absent.

Confusion gave way to relief as she realized that the blood, the demanding voices—they had all been part of a horrifying dream. But the relief was short-lived, the echo of the voice that had boomed so commandingly in her nightmare still rang in her ears: "Give us the girl, and you are free to go."

Her hands trembled as she reached out to gently shake John awake. "Wake up," she whispered urgently, her voice shaky.

John's eyes flickered open, immediately alert to the tone of distress in her voice. "Sweetheart? What's wrong?"

Mary's words tumbled out in a rush; the fear evident in her tone. "The voices, the blood—they said they wanted Emma..."

John quickly oriented himself, his gaze sweeping the dimly lit room. Seeing no immediate threat, he turned his full attention back to Mary. "There's nothing here. It was just a nightmare. We're still here, just us. And we're safe for now, except... except for Ben."

Mary scanned the room, her eyes lingering on the empty spaces where Ben might have played or sat. The realization that it had been a dream did little to calm her nerves. The details had been so vivid, so terrifyingly real. "But it felt so real. I heard it... I saw it," she insisted, her voice tinged with the residue of terror.

John wrapped his arms around Mary, pulling her close in an attempt to comfort her, though his own heart was heavy with dread. He felt the tremble in her body as she leaned into him, her fears palpable between them. "It's okay, sweets," he whispered softly, his voice steady despite the turmoil churning inside him. "It was just a dream. We're all here, safe."

"Babe, I can't tell what's real anymore," Mary whispered, her voice thick with desperation. She clung to the fragile hope that everything they'd endured was just a prolonged nightmare. "Maybe Ben isn't really gone. Maybe those girls never appeared... and these voices—it's all in my head," she murmured, more to herself than to John. Despite the gnawing fear that told her otherwise, she prayed fervently that the terrifying events were just figments of her imagination.

As he held her, John's mind raced with the eerie accuracy of Mary's recent nightmares, which had begun to align disturbingly with their reality. Even though part of him wanted to dismiss it all as coincidence, the mounting evidence was becoming harder to ignore. He looked down into her eyes, seeing the flicker of terror and recognition that what she dreamed might yet come to pass.

"You've been right before," he admitted, his voice barely above a whisper, acknowledging the unspoken truth between them. "Your dreams... they're not just dreams, are they?"

Mary's eyes met his, filled with a mix of fear and a pleading for understanding. "I don't know, John, but I'm scared of what might happen next."

John tightened his embrace, a protective gesture but also one of solidarity. "Whatever comes, we'll face it together. You're not alone in this. We're together, and we'll keep Emma safe, too. That's what matters now. I won't let these voices win."

At that moment, a bond of trust and mutual reliance was fortified. John's words weren't just to soothe Mary; they were a vow—a commitment to stand by her side, facing whatever strange tides were turning around them.

As John spoke, Mary felt a mix of relief and guilt wash over her. Relief that Emma was safe beside her, and profound guilt over Ben's unknown fate. They were not all safe, not yet.

They resettled themselves in the living room. John stayed awake, keeping watch while Mary tried to rest with Emma nestled beside her.

The night dragged on, each hour stretching out endlessly. The house remained quiet, almost as if it were holding its breath, waiting for the first light of dawn to expose its secrets. In the oppressive silence, every small noise seemed amplified—a testament to the heightened state of alert they were forced to maintain.

As they waited for the morning, the boundary between nightmare and reality blurred, the darkness of the night intertwining with the shadows of their fears. They were together, yet each felt the isolation that terror brings, facing an unseen, unfathomable adversary that seemed as much a part of the house as the wood and nails that held it together.

Mary, her nerves frayed to their breaking point, listened as the voices began to articulate more clearly, each word dripping with pure evil. "Ben is with us," they hissed, their tone mockingly gentle. "He's happy here. He wants you to join him, Emma."

Emma, her eyes wide with a mixture of fear and longing, clutched her mother's hand tighter. "Mommy, is Ben really happy?" she asked, her voice quivering.

Mary pulled her daughter close, her own heart aching with the knowledge of the voices' deceit. "No, sweetheart, they're lying. We can't listen to them," she whispered fiercely.

The voices laughed, a chilling sound that seemed to reverberate through the very foundation of the house. "Poor little Emma, missing her brother. Wouldn't you like to see him again? Come to us, and you'll be together forever."

John rose abruptly, anger flashing in his eyes as he faced the direction of the disembodied voices. "Enough!" he shouted, his voice echoing defiantly in the oppressive air. "Fuck you! You're not taking anyone else from us!"

The house seemed to recoil at his words, and then, with a sudden, violent energy, a force unseen struck John. He was thrown back against the wall, his head hitting with a sickening thud. He slid to the floor, unconscious, a dark silence enveloping him.

Mary screamed, rushing to his side, her hands shaking as she checked for any sign of injury. "John!" she cried, panic-stricken, but he was unresponsive, his breathing shallow.

In the chaos, Emma's resolve shattered. Tears streaming down her face, she turned towards the door. "Just take me!" she screamed, her voice breaking. "I-Im ready to be with my brother now!" With those heart-wrenching words, she bolted out the front door into the darkness.

Mary, torn between her unconscious husband and her fleeing daughter, hesitated, a moment of indecision that felt like an eternity. "Emma!" she cried out, despair gripping her heart.

As she ran to the doorway, a new horror greeted her. From the ceiling of the hallway, blood began to drip, slow at first, then gaining in volume, a gruesome rainfall that seemed to answer Emma's desperate declaration. "Here is a dear piece of your son," the voices hissed spitefully.

Frozen with horror, Mary looked up at the blood-soaked ceiling, her mind racing. The reality of their situation was ridiculous, the house seemingly alive with the spirit of their tormentors. But amidst the terror, a fierce determination ignited within her. She would not let this malicious force win.

She dragged John to a safer spot away from the blood, propping him against the wall, and then dashed outside after Emma. The cold air hit her like a slap as she called out into the night, her voice desperate. "Emma! Stop!"

Her daughter was a small figure, silhouetted against the moonlit path, hesitating as her mother's call reached her. The house behind them groaned and creaked, as if angered by Mary's resistance.

Breathing heavily, Mary caught up to Emma, grabbing her firmly by the shoulders. "We are not giving in to them," she said, her voice firm despite the fear. "We will find a way to get Ben back, and we will fight whatever this is, together."

Emma, sobbing, nodded, clinging to her mother as they stood under the vast, uncaring sky.

Emma and Mary ambled back to the house and up the front stairs. Once inside they noticed that John was coming to.

Mary and Emma both rushed over to him and held him tight.

As the Harpers huddled together in the room, the unsettling silence was shattered by the sound of footsteps on the porch. Heartbeats quickened as the doorknob rattled violently under the force of someone—or something—trying to gain entry. The door held firm, but the eerie silence that followed was soon broken by a chilling voice, sing-song and menacing.

"Come on, Emma. Your brother is out here with us. Come play in the woods with us," taunted the voice, its tone mockingly sweet yet dripping with malice. Laughter followed, dark and twisted, as the unseen figures began to sing a distorted version of "Ring Around the Rosie." The stomping of their feet on the wooden porch boards created a perverse rhythm as if they were dancing in some sort of evil celebration.

Suddenly, the laughter escalated into a frenzied scream. The sound of a heavy object being lifted was quickly followed by a crash as a rock hurtled through the window, shattering the glass and spraying shards across the room. "Give us the fucking girl!" the voice yelled, turning the nightmarish scene into one of outright terror.

Inside, John's resolve snapped. "Enough of this shit," he muttered furiously, moving towards the door, only to find it jammed or locked from the outside. As he struggled with the door, a face appeared through the broken window—a young girl's face, grotesquely smiling, her skin sliced open by the jagged glass. "Ah, ah, John, don't get yourself hurt now," she cooed menacingly. "Just give us the girl, and we'll leave."

"You're not getting my damn daughter!" John shot back, his voice a mix of anger and defiance.

The girl's laugh was chilling as she withdrew her bloodied face from the window, leaving a trail of blood dripping down to the sill. "Well, let's have some more fun then," she cackled, her voice echoing into the night.

The Harpers retreated from the window, the reality of their situation settling in with a heavy, sickening thud. They were under siege, trapped in their own home by forces that seemed to delight in their fear. They would not submit, they would not break. They needed a plan, a way to protect themselves and to fight back.

The darkness outside the Harper's shelter teemed with malevolent energy as the figures orchestrated their twisted games. Silhouettes darted back and forth across the jagged opening where the window once protected them, each movement deliberate and menacing.

In a grotesque display, one shadow detached from the dance, hurling an object through the remaining sliver of glass. It landed with a thud at John's feet—a small, stuffed bear, unmistakably Ben's, now dirt-streaked and partially torn. The toy, once a symbol of innocence, lay as a ghastly token of the night's terror.

Outside, the figures resumed their frightening play. They dragged two large dolls across the wooden porch; the figures were crudely dressed in Ben and Emma's clothes, their limbs jerking in a shocking mimicry of life. The dolls' glassy eyes and slack expressions mocked the family's anguish as they thudded against the house, leaves and twigs catching in their hair.

A voice, too cheerful to belong to the night, sang out a lullaby, each note hanging twisted and wrong in the cool air. It was joined by laughter—sharp, disjointed sounds that seemed to slice through the stillness. As the song reached its crescendo, the dolls were hoisted up, dangled from nooses made of garden twine, swinging from the porch railing like vile puppets.

The most harrowing scene unfolded as one figure stepped into the faint light cast by the dying lamps inside. It paraded in a circle, dragging its feet in a mock dance around the dolls. Its voice rose in a sing-song chant, "Ring around the Rosie, a pocket full of posies," before breaking into peals of laughter that sounded too much like sobbing.

Without warning, the dance stopped. The figure's head turned sharply towards the house, its features obscured but its intent horrifyingly clear. With a swift motion, it snatched the dolls down, their heads snapping back with a grotesque crack. It then flung them with force against the side of the house, where they hit with dull thuds, leaving smears of dark, wet mud on the siding.

As the first pale light of dawn began to infiltrate the sky, the ominous chorus and dance waned, retreating into the shadows from which they had emerged. The figures vanished, leaving behind a yard strewn with the nightmarish remnants of their visit—Ben's toy, the defiled dolls, and an unspoken threat hanging as heavy as the morning mist.

THREADS OF THE PAST

As the day marched on, the sunlight filtered through the trees and spilled a muted glow into the somber shadows of their surroundings. Emerging cautiously from their makeshift sanctuary, the Harper family faced the new day with wary eyes. Morning had swiftly transitioned into afternoon, and while the air remained crisp, it was heavy with the echoes of the previous night's terror. Yet, in the light of day, John, Mary, and Emma found a reluctant courage stirring within them.

They decided it was time to call for help. Mary picked up the phone to dial 911, but the line was dead. Puzzled and increasingly anxious, John rushed outside to check the line and found it had been cleanly cut—a deliberate act.

The reality of their isolation sank in, and a heavy silence fell over them.

"Let's drive into town," John suggested, retrieving his spare car key with a glint of hope. He went out to check the car, his movements hurried and tense.

Outside, as John reached under the dash to check the wiring, the intrusive whispers returned, coaxing him to pull at the wires. "They don't need to leave... they belong here," the voices murmured insidiously. With a shaking hand and a heavy heart, John tampered with the car's wiring, ensuring it wouldn't start.

Returning inside, John faced his family with a grave expression. "The car won't turn over. It looks like they got to it too," he lied, the guilt gnawing at him but overshadowed by the compelling voices in his head.

Mary's eyes filled with frustration and fear. "We're cut off, aren't we?" she murmured, her voice cracking under the strain.

The walk to town was far too long and dangerous to attempt. Faced with no other options, they resolved to clean up their home and fortify it against further intrusions.

"We'll take a stand, right here," John declared, his voice firm, trying to mask his internal turmoil. "We'll make this place safe, and figure this out together."

The family set to work, their actions driven by a mix of determination and desperation, each trying to ignore the sinking feeling that they were playing right into a darker plan.

They moved through the house with a renewed sense of purpose, determined to unearth any clues that might help them find Ben or understand the malevolent forces at play.

Throughout the day, the living room bore silent witness to the chaos of the previous night, its floor strewn with glass shards that glittered sharply under the afternoon light. John moved methodically, examining each fragment and displaced item, his actions precise yet heavy with quiet desperation. Beside him, Emma worked with a determined calm, her youthful face set in concentration as she helped shift cushions and rearrange the lighter furniture, each movement meticulous and deliberate.

The family spent hours trying to restore some semblance of order. John took on the task of cleaning the yard, picking up the scattered debris and glass, his movements automatic. He found an old piece of plywood in the shed and used it to cover the broken window, sealing off the cold air that whispered through the jagged opening.

Inside, Mary tackled the interior with equal parts determination and sorrow. She swept up the remnants of broken glass, righted the upturned furniture, and sorted through the contents of drawers that had been haphazardly searched. Her resolve faltered when she reached Ben's room. The sight of her young son's violated space was overwhelming; toys displaced, clothes strewn about, a stark reminder of the night's terror. Tears streamed down her cheeks as she slowly tidied up, each item she restored a painful reminder of the security they had lost. The idea that someone could invade this personal sanctuary and threaten her child was a reality too cruel to bear fully.

Together, they moved through the motions of cleaning and repairing, each task a small step against the tide of fear and uncertainty that had swept into their lives. As the day wore on, the physical evidence of the intrusion was gradually erased, but the emotional scars ran deep, leaving the family bound together in a shared vigilance, wary of the shadows that now seemed too deep, too filled with potential threats.

Mary ventured alone into the basement, the air growing cooler as she descended. The basement was cluttered with the past—a collection of boxes filled with family memorabilia, old furniture covered in sheets, and shelves buckling under the weight of dusty books and forgotten albums. As she moved through the space, her hands brushed against the cold concrete and cobweb-laced corners, her fingers tracing the spines of books in search of anything that felt out of the ordinary.

Her search was methodical, fueled by sheer determination. Behind stacks of old newspapers and moth-eaten clothing, her hand finally made contact with something unexpected. It was a small, leather-bound journal, tucked away behind a row of aged encyclopedias. The cover was worn, the pages yellowed with age, but it was what was written inside that caused her breath to catch.

As Mary carefully turned the fragile pages of the ancient journal, her hands trembling slightly, she discovered a

chilling account that cast a shadow over the warm memories of Harold, the town's once-beloved figure. According
to the journal, Harold had been a gentle and generous
man, beloved by all, throughout his life until a devastating
event turned the town against him.

The entries detailed how, in a swift and cruel twist of
fate, Harold was accused of kidnapping local children—a
crime he vehemently denied but which ignited the townsfolk's fear into a violent fervor. Despite his protests and
lack of evidence, the community's grief and paranoia cul-
minated in a dark act of vengeance: Harold was con-
demned to die at the stake. As the flames rose, Harold,
betrayed and consumed by the injustice, cursed the town
and its inhabitants, vowing vengeance from beyond the
grave.

Harold's death marked the beginning of a series of
hauntings and misfortunes that plagued the town, which
he orchestrated as spectral manipulations from the after-
life. The journal hinted that the spirit of Harold, twisted
by his cruel death, found ways to perpetuate his presence
and influence, turning his once benign interventions into
a sinister legacy.

It spoke of rituals conducted deep within the tunnels
beneath his estate, where Harold's spirit attempted to harness and commune with the 'spirits of the woods'—en-
tities he believed empowered him to exact his revenge on
the townsfolk who had wronged him. These practices were
not just attempts at contact but were steeped in a belief

that through them, Harold could transcend his earthly bounds and enact retribution on a grand scale.

The journal, written by someone who seemed to have been close to Harold, perhaps a confidant or family member, painted a vivid picture of a man transformed by the town's betrayal from a figure of kindness to a vengeful ghost, manipulating events and people from beyond the veil. The detailed accounts included sketches of the hidden tunnel system and descriptions of eerie ceremonies aimed at binding Harold's spirit to the physical world, ensuring his presence remained active and malevolent.

The realization that they were caught in a cycle of an ancient vendetta was terrifying. Yet, knowing the origin of their torment provided them with a grim clarity. If they were to have any hope of saving Ben and themselves, they needed to confront the heart of this darkness, to venture into the very tunnels that Harold had crafted, and face whatever horrors lay in wait.

With the journal clutched tightly to her chest, Mary hurried back upstairs and presented the journal, laying it on the coffee table like a relic.

"Where the hell did you find that," John looked over at Mary with a puzzled expression on his face.

"In the basement, behind the old books," Mary announced, her voice a mix of excitement and dread. "It talks about the house, about something hidden here—something old and very dangerous."

As John and Emma listened, a heavy silence filled the room, broken only by the crackle of the old pages as Mary turned them. The tale was not just history; it was a mirror reflecting their current nightmare, suggesting that the malevolent force they now faced was not just a remnant of Harold but a continuation of a curse he had invited upon himself and the house.

Understanding dawned painfully on the Harpers. The voices, the visions of children, the incessant whistling—they were all manifestations of Harold's legacy, a tapestry of torment woven from his unresolved wrath and the dark energies he had stirred. The house, with its hidden passages and echoes of past horrors, was not just a structure; it had become a living, breathing entity of Harold's making, ensnaring them as it had so many before.

John and Emma leaned closer, their eyes wide as Mary flipped through the pages, showing them passages that mirrored their own terrifying experiences. The realization that they were living in a house with such a dark past, and perhaps haunted by more than just memories, settled over them like a cold shroud.

Mary's voice trembled as she delved into the most disturbing aspects of the journal, revealing Harold Harper's sadistic practices in excruciating detail. The night felt heavier as she described the depths of cruelty that once permeated the walls of their home.

Mary recounted a passage from the journal that revealed a harrowing aspect of Harold's legacy. "Harold became a master of manipulation, both psychological and spiritual. His expertise lay in infiltrating the senses and minds of those within his domain," she read, a chill running through her as the words sank in.

"The journal describes how Harold's spirit would weave itself into the consciousness of those in the house, often without their awareness. He would instill a pervasive darkness that clouded both vision and judgment, creating an atmosphere thick with dread. This darkness was not just physical but psychological, stripping away any sense of safety and replacing it with ceaseless terror."

Mary continued, her voice barely above a whisper, "He didn't need to physically blindfold his victims; his presence alone was enough to blind them to reality. They would hear his voice—whispers, screams, the soft deceit of comfort—each sound meticulously crafted to fray their nerves."

The text detailed further how Harold's spirit induced hallucinations and delusions, forcing his captives to see and do horrific things to themselves and each other, all under the guise of escaping their fears. "These torments were designed to break the will, to make his victims his unwitting pawns, acting out in desperation under the illusion of his orchestration."

As the implications of Harold's methods dawned on them, John, Mary, and Emma grasped the true nature of their tormentor. The eerie events they had experienced—the unseen voices, the oppressive atmosphere, the mysterious disappearances—were not just remnants of a troubled past. They were the manipulations of Harold's vengeful spirit, reaching from beyond the grave to control and consume them.

"The spirit of Harold doesn't just haunt this place; he infests it, bending reality to his will, making us see and believe things that drive us to the brink," Mary concluded, closing the journal with a sense of dread. The reality that their minds could be turned against them was a revelation far more terrifying than any ghostly apparition.

John looked between Mary and Emma, his face set with resolve but his eyes betraying a flicker of fear. "We're dealing with something that doesn't just want to scare us; it wants to use us, control us like puppets," he said, his voice steady despite the growing fear. "We have to fight not just for Ben, but against losing ourselves to this... this manipulation."

The room grew colder as they acknowledged the depth of Harold's intrusion into their lives, understanding that their battle was as much against their minds as it was against the malevolent spirit that sought to corrupt them.

As Mary described these atrocities, a chilling picture of Harold Harper emerged—not just a recluse, but a methodical torturer who reveled in the control and subjugation of his captives. His experiments weren't just acts of random cruelty but a systematic attempt to break the human spirit, to transform people into subservient shadows of their former selves, conditioned to carry out his macabre whims all in the name of revenge.

As Mary finished reading, a heavy silence enveloped the room, thick with the grim details of Harold Harper's past. The air seemed to thicken, charged with the weight of her words.

"Babe," Mary said, her voice low and urgent, "did you ever hear of a relative named Harold?" Her gaze was intent on his face, searching for any flicker of recognition. "Could it be that he somehow drew us here from the city? In some sick, twisted way, does he want us to inherit his horrific legacy?"

John's voice softened a hint of nostalgia mingling with the growing tension. "My grandmother used to tell me tales of Harold Harper when I was a boy," he began, his gaze distant as he recalled the story. "She painted him as a kind man, loved and respected by everyone in Micaville. He was like a guardian to the town, always helping out where he could."

He sighed; the memories tinged with the wisdom of hindsight. "But things turned sour. The town turned against him and blamed him for things he didn't do. At the stake, as the flames rose, he swore vengeance against those who wronged him, promising that their descendants would never find peace."

John looked around the shadow-filled room, his story hanging in the air. "I thought it was just a spooky story, meant to scare a kid at bedtime. I always thought she was just trying to teach me some kind of life lesson about not letting people take your kindness for weakness. But now, it seems like there might have been some truth to her tales."

The notion that this malevolent ancestor might have influenced their move to this cursed place unnerved him deeply. "Perhaps he's never really left," Mary continued, her voice steady despite the dread that filled it. "Maybe he's woven into the very essence of this house, the land, entwining his presence with every leaf and stone. And now, he's reaching out to us, pulling us into his nightmare."

The realization that they might be enmeshed in the will of a long-dead man, intent on perpetuating his vile deeds through them, was chilling. As they processed the horrifying implications, the necessity of finding a way out became clear. Yet, escaping the legacy of Harold Harper would be no small feat. The unfolding story seemed determined to draw them deeper into its dark heart, challenging them to either confront the past or be consumed by it.

John finally spoke, his voice a mix of anger and frustration. "We need to keep searching this house. There must be something more, someplace where he gets into these secret tunnels. We have to find it—understand it—to have any chance of ending this nightmare. Maybe Ben is down there right now."

The Harper family's quest had taken a darker turn, the journal not just a guide but a warning: the depths of human cruelty knew no bounds, and they were now caught in a legacy of darkness that threatened to engulf them just as it had those before them.

Mary continued to relay the harrowing details from the journal, her voice growing firmer as she pieced together the past horrors with their current ordeal. "Harper's manipulation didn't end at the threshold of this house," she said, turning another aged page. "He forced those under his control to venture out under the cover of night, stealing from the unsuspecting townsfolk who mistook them for phantoms of the forest."

"The locals, bound by their superstitions, believed that not whistling after dark and leaving offerings on their porches would keep the spirits at bay. And it worked, in a way, keeping them safe from Harper's puppets who roamed the woods," Mary explained.

Night was once again closing in on them and if they were to have a chance to survive, they would need to find a way to fight back. The three of them made their way back down to the basement in search of more answers. John paced back and forth, his mind racing. "This guy, Harper, he concocted a reign of terror so complete, he had the whole town fooled. There must be a door, a hidden passage we've missed," he speculated, looking around the dimly lit room as if the answer might reveal itself on the walls.

"Maybe it leads to that old tunnel system the journal hinted at, somewhere out in the woods," John mused, turning to look out the window at the expansive property that stretched out around their home.

Emma, her face shadowed by the room's dim light, spoke up with a tremor in her voice, "Could it still be out there? Could that be where Ben is now?"

"It's entirely possible," John answered, his voice tinged with a mix of hope and dread. "If Harper's setup was as extensive as this journal makes it out to be, he'd need a secluded spot to keep his operations well hidden. An abandoned mineshaft would be perfect—hidden from prying eyes, difficult to access, and even harder to escape from."

In the dim, flickering lightbulb of the basement, John and Mary's breaths came in hurried gasps, their eyes wide with a mixture of hope and terror. The voice of their son, Ben, echoed through the old, musty air, a chilling blend of desperation and eerie joy. "Mom, Dad, I'm outside. Please help me," he called, his words followed by that disturbing, contagious laughter that seemed to crawl under their skin.

Seized by a frantic urgency, John and Mary climbed the creaking stairs, the shadows thrown by the light warping around them like dark spirits in flight. Emma, clung to her mother's hand, her small face pale in the ghostly light. But as they neared the top, the voice—Ben's voice, twisted and echoing as if from a great distance—disoriented them, and in a heart-stopping moment, Emma's hand slipped away.

The house seemed to pulse with a spiteful life of its own. The walls groaned, and the air grew oppressively cold as they burst through the door leading out of the basement.

"Emma!" Mary cried out, terror pitching her voice higher. But the house swallowed the sound, the silence as thick as fog.

Without knowing, in their desperate rush to the front door, they had left Emma behind. Unseen by her frantic parents, she wandered, drawn by the spectral echo of her brother's laughter toward the back door. It swung open as if welcoming her into the night, and she stepped through, leaving her parents behind.

Outside, the woods loomed like a dark wall, impenetrable and foreboding. Emma, caught in the evil will of the entity that haunted them, moved as though in a trance, her small figure disappearing among the gnarled trees that seemed to whisper and hiss her name.

John and Mary, realizing too late their grave mistake, turned back from the threshold of the front door. Their home, once a sanctuary, now felt like a labyrinth designed by madness itself. They retraced their steps, calling for Emma, their voices desperate, fueling the thick silence that now enveloped the house.

As they reached the back door, the night air hit them and forced them to take a step back. The door stood ominously open, a dark maw leading to the unknown. The woods called to them; an opus of night sounds that masked the soft footsteps of their daughter being swallowed by the dark.

Now, deep in the heart of the woods, Emma's form was just a shadow, flitting between the darker shades of the trees. The forest around her seemed alive, branches moving with disturbing intent, the ground beneath her feet whispering of pure evil.

John and Mary stumbled into the night, their every breath a white cloud in the chill air. They plunged into the darkness after their daughter, the house behind them silent. As they moved further from the light of their home, they realized the horrifying truth: the house had not just isolated them—it had orchestrated this nightmare, pulling them apart, weaving their terror into the fabric of its dark history.

In the icy grip of fear, they pressed on, the reality of their situation setting like frost in their veins. Emma was out there, alone in the clutch of an unspeakable evil, and they were ensnared in a horror that was only beginning to unfold.

THE SHADOWS OF FATHER

U nder the spell that seemed to dance through the gnarled trees of the Appalachian wilderness, Emma's steps were silent against the forest floor, guided by unseen forces. The night was alive with the haunting rustle of leaves and an ominous chill that seeped into her bones. The forest rearranged itself with each step she took, drawing her deeper into its shadowy embrace.

In the clearing, bathed in ghostly moonlight, Ben and one of the girls danced, their shadows entwining amidst the underbrush. Ben's laughter, joyous yet haunting, filled the air as he twirled his companion. The scene had a surreal quality, like a distorted fairy tale, where the prince was not quite himself.

Emma, drawn by the sight of her brother, stepped cautiously into the clearing. Her heart leaped with a mixture of joy and trepidation as she saw Ben's bright smile, though his eyes betrayed an unsettling emptiness. Pushing her concerns aside, she moved closer, her footsteps soft on the forest floor, hoping to join their dance and bring Ben back.

Just as she reached out to touch Ben, reveling in the familiarity of her brother's presence, the second girl emerged from the shadows like a wraith. Emma, caught off guard by the sudden appearance, barely registered the movement before feeling a sharp, stunning blow to the back of her head. As she collapsed to the ground, consciousness fading, the last thing she heard was the eerie sound of Ben's laughter mingling with the girl's singsong voices, repeating a haunting rhyme as they danced around her fallen form. The last thing she heard was the girls whispering something about taking her to the cave, where Father would keep her as his own.

Emma blinked, struggling to focus as her eyes adjusted to the dim, flickering light of what looked like a cave. The cold, damp air filled her lungs, bringing her to a full sense of awareness. Beside her, Ben sat hunched, his knees drawn up to his chest, his eyes wide with a palpable fear that was a stark contrast to the joyous laughter she had witnessed moments before in the clearing.

"Ben?" Emma's voice was shaky, her mind racing to piece together the situation. "What's happening? Why are we here?"

Ben turned his head slowly towards her, his expression haunted. "I... I don't really know, Emma," he murmured, his voice trembling. "The girls—they brought me here. They say I have to stay. They watch me all the time. I'm so, so s-scared Sis."

Emma reached out, taking his small, cold hand in hers, trying to offer some comfort. "Why didn't you come back with us, Ben? We looked for you everywhere."

Ben's eyes flickered with the shadows cast by the torchlight, his next words spilling out in a rush. "It-It's the voices, Emma. Th-they come into my head. They tell me things... scary things. They told me I can't go home yet. They say I have to stay and be part of their family now."

"Voices?" Emma's heart sank as she realized the gravity of her brother's words. The whimsical dance in the clearing wasn't joy—it was manipulation, something controlling him, making him act out of character.

"They're always talking, and when they talk, it feels like I'm not myself anymore," Ben continued, his small hands clutching at his head as if trying to physically block out the voices. "I try to tell them to go away, but they don't listen. They say they're my family now. But I want to come home, Emma. I'm scared. Are we d-dreaming right now?"

Emma squeezed his hand tighter, her protective instincts as his older sister kicking in. "We'll get out of here,

Ben. I promise. We'll go home together." Her mind raced, considering their options, the urgency to escape more pressing than ever.

"D-do you hear that, Ben?

"I don't hear anything, Sis. All I keep hearing is these voices in my head."

"I heard Mom and Dad! They're looking for us!" Emma's voice cracked as panic rose within her, the sound of their distant calls fueling her fear.

"Mom! Dad! We're down here!" Emma's shouts echoed off the stone walls, the sound bouncing back to them, hollow and ghostly.

Their parents' voices responded, desperate and close, yet agonizingly out of reach. "Emma! Ben! Keep talking, we're coming!"

Ben's eyes were wide with fright as he pulled closer to his sister. "Emma, this place—it's not just a cave. There's something here with us, something old and dark from the mountains. He says his name is Harold, but the girls call it 'Father'—they told me it's been here forever, watching."

A shiver ran down Emma's spine as she held her brother closer. The name seemed to seep into the walls around them, the air growing colder with each mention.

"We found a journal back in the house and I think this Harold guy is our relative. The house we live in used to be his."

"Emma, it seems like the whispers are coming from everywhere. When it talks, it's like it's in my head, like it has control of me.

In the shadowy confines of the mineshaft, Ben clung to Emma, his small voice trembled as he recounted the horrors imposed by the eerie figures. His words were halting, filled with fear and revulsion.

Emma's stomach turned as Ben's words spilled out, each one heavier than the last. "Emma, it was gross," he murmured, his small body trembling next to hers. "They hurt animals... and it was so blood-bloody. They laughed, Emma. They made me help them. I didn't want to, b-b-but they wouldn't take no for an answer." His voice broke, haunted by the memories.

He glanced around nervously as if the shadows might be listening. "They steal food from people's homes at night. We didn't find any last night, and... and they caught a raccoon. They did terrible things to it and then—they made me eat some of it, Emma. It wasn't cooked or anything."

The horror of his experience was etched deep into his eyes, a stark reminder of the nightmare they were living. Emma wrapped her arms tighter around him, fighting back her horror and disgust, focusing instead on the need to protect her little brother. "We're going to get out of here, Ben," she assured him with a fierceness that belied her fear. "We're going to make sure they can't do this to anyone else, okay? I'm here now, and I won't let them hurt you anymore."

He paused, taking a shaky breath before continuing. "And they took me out to our house last night. I don't remember all of it; it's like parts of my mind are just... just gone. I was there, but it wasn't really me. It's like I was watching myself from somewhere else, doing things... I can't even... I just don't know."

Emma began crying listening to her poor baby brother talk, her heart aching for him. "What do you mean, Ben? What did they make you do?"

Ben's eyes were haunted as he tried to articulate the foggy memories. "I was outside our house, moving around in the dark. They had me do things—strange things. I think I was looking for ways to get in, or maybe... maybe leaving things. It's all a blur, Emma. I remember feeling scared and confused like I was trapped in a bad dream. Like a nightmare."

His voice grew more fearful as he recalled the shadowy figures' manipulation. "They control everything, Emma. When they tell you to do something, you just... do it. It's like your body isn't yours anymore."

Emma tightened her grip on her brother's hand yet again, fighting to keep her fear in check as she listened to him describe the unthinkable. "Oh, Ben, that-that's terrible. I'm so sorry you had to do those things," she murmured, her voice thick with emotion.

Ben's eyes widened with fear as he huddled closer to Emma. "And there's more," he said, his voice barely above a whisper. "They... they have this room where they do really scary stuff to each other. They use knives and hot stuff an d... and they hurt themselves. Then they make things like necklaces out of...out of what they did." His face contorted with the weight of what he'd seen.

"They wear them like trophies," he added, shuddering. "They say that Father is going to make me do it too. I think he controls them, Emma. When I look in their eyes, it's like nobody's there. It's really creepy. I feel sorry for them, but I'm so, so scared too."

He paused, struggling to breathe as he remembered the horrors. "They want to make me do things like that to someone tonight. They said if I don't, I'll be the one they do those things to next. I'm really sc-scared, Emma."

Emma pulled her brother into a protective embrace, her heart racing with a fierce determination to shield him from any more horror. "We're going to get out of here, Ben," she assured him with a firmness she hoped was convincing. "We're not going to let them do anything to you. We'll find a way to escape, I promise."

The sound of distant footsteps echoed faintly, a grim reminder of the immediate danger they still faced. Emma glanced around, her mind racing for a plan, her brother's fearful face driving her resolve.

"Stay close to me, no matter what," she instructed softly. "As soon as we get a chance, we're going to run for it, straight back to the house. We'll find a place to hide and then figure out how to get help."

Ben nodded, wiping away tears with the back of his hand, his trust in his sister complete. Together, they huddled closer in the shadows, waiting for the opportune moment to make their escape, each minute stretching into eternity as they braced for what might come next, but nothing came.

"How do we get out, Ben? What did it tell you?" Emma's voice was urgent, her mind racing for solutions.

Ben shook his head, his face pale in the torchlight. "I don't know. It... they—just laugh and say we shouldn't have let it in. It's like whatever this is, is enjoying watching us get scared. We might be..." His voice trailed off, unable to finish the thought.

Emma felt a surge of protectiveness over her younger brother. "Don't worry, I-I'm here, we'll find a way. Well find a way together," she whispered, trying to sound braver than she felt.

Their voices continued to echo up to their parents, a lifeline made of sound. Meanwhile, Emma and Ben huddled together in the dark, the oppressive presence of Father watching from the shadows, its intentions as mysterious and terrifying as the ancient legends themselves.

In the suffocating darkness of the cave, Emma and Ben sat together shivering in the cold night air, their breaths shallow and rapid as the distant sounds of chaos erupted above them. The cave's cold embrace seemed to tighten around them with every scream that filtered through the earthen ceiling—a gruesome symphony of their parents' torment.

Emma tried to call out to her parents again but there was no response. They both began crying their thoughts going to the deepest corners of their imagination.

"Emma, they-they have them now! Th-they took our p-parents!" Ben said as he looked over at his sobbing sister, his eyes vacant as a small smile began building on his face.

Above, in the decrepit basement of the old house, John and Mary were caught in a nightmarish scene. Invisible forces manipulated the shadows, crafting tendrils of darkness that slithered across the walls and floor. John was thrown against the rough stone wall, his arms pinned by shadowy limbs that felt like cold iron. Each struggle brought a sharper, more excruciating pain as the spectral bindings tightened, crushing his wrists and ankles, and drawing small streams of blood that dripped to the dusty floor.

Mary, equally ensnared, was suspended in midair, her feet dangling helplessly. The shadows around her morphed into grotesque forms, whispering horrors only she could hear. One form—a darker, denser shadow—approached her, its edges flickering like the flame of a candle. It reached into her mouth, silencing her screams, as it began to pull, stretch, and twist her jaw in a grotesque display. The sound of cracking bones mingled with the muffled cries trying to escape.

Below, Ben pressed his hands against his ears, trying to block out the relentless assault of their parents' screams, but the sound seemed to vibrate through the very ground, resonating inside his skull. Emma wrapped her arms around him, her own body shaking as tears streamed down her face. Each cry from above punctured the heavy silence of the cave and splintered her heart.

"Mom! Dad!" Emma's voice cracked as she shouted, her plea swallowed by the oppressive darkness of the cave. The only response was an increase in the intensity of the screams—a clear, cruel signal that her cries had been heard but only served to inspire further torment for her parents.

Ben's expression turned serious as he leaned closer to Emma. "Sis, it's like, all the time," he murmured, his young voice tinged with confusion and fear. "I don't even know if it's real anymore or just... just something messing with my head. It's like it's pulling me away from what's real. I can't even tell if the stuff happening to them is actually happening, or if it's just... just in my mind."

The cave around them felt alive, feeding off the terror that seeped down from the house. The shadows near the siblings began to stir, whispering in a chorus of disjointed voices, mocking their helplessness and delighting in their despair. The dark presence of Father, materialized briefly before them, its form nebulous and shifting, eyes glowing with a malevolent glee.

"We feed on your fear," it hissed, its voice a mix of glee and malice. "Your pain is the root, the heart of this land. You belong to it now, as do they."

Above, the torture escalated. John's cries became hoarse, gargling sounds and the horrific tableau was too much for Ben. He broke down completely, his young mind unable to process the brutal assault on his senses. Emma, though wracked with grief and fear, drew him close, her lips pressed against his ear, whispering empty reassurances. "I'm here, Ben. I'm here," she sobbed, her voice barely audible over the chorus of their parents' agony and the sinister laughter of Father.

As the final echoes of their parents' suffering filled the cave, the overwhelming horror proved too much for their young minds. Emma's grip on Ben loosened as the darkness seemed to swirl and consume them, their consciousness slipping away under the crushing weight of despair and fear. Together, they succumbed to the darkness, passing out, lost in the malevolent embrace of its wretched control.

WHISPERS FROM THE DEEP

B en's eyes snapped open to the sound of his sister's anguished cry piercing the stifling darkness of the cave. "Why are you doing this to us?" Emma's voice was hoarse, filled with a blend of fear and desperation. Her nightmare had been vivid, too real, echoing with the screams and cries of their parents under torture.

Ben, jolted awake by the terror in Emma's voice, immediately started crying out in panic. "M-Mommy, Daddy, can you hear us?" His voice was small and shaky, echoing off the cold, damp walls that surrounded them.

Up above, amidst the musty silence of the old house's basement, John and Mary's voices cut through the darkness, reaching their children below. "Ben... Emma, don't worry, we are going to find a way to get you out," Mary called down, her voice a mixture of determination and comforting warmth.

Hearing their parents alive and unharmed, Emma felt a momentary relief wash over her, but it was quickly clouded by confusion. She clung to Ben, her mind racing. The horrors they had heard—could it have been just a nightmare?

"Mom, it was awful," Emma's voice trembled as she recounted the dream. "We heard you... you were being hurt."

Ben's voice trembled as he listened to his parents through the floor above, trying to grasp the gravity of their situation. But the weight of their predicament bore heavily on him. His eyes darted around the shadowy cave, seeking any hint of escape when a faint light glimmered in the distance. "Emma, look! We can get out of here," he exclaimed, a small hope breaking through his fear.

Before Emma could respond, Ben took off running towards the light. His sister's heart sank with dread. "Ben, no! It's just Harold!" Emma screamed, her voice echoing through the cavernous tunnels.

But Ben was already far ahead, the light seemingly flickering and retreating as he ran, drawing him deeper into an endless labyrinth of twisting tunnels that stretched on for miles. With each step, the light moved further away, pulling him into the depths of a deceptive trap set by Harold.

Above, in the basement, John heard Emma's fading screams. Panic seized him, and he bolted outside, desperate for any tool that might aid their rescue. His eyes caught sight of a pickaxe leaning against a tree. With no time to lose, he grabbed it and rushed back to the basement, where he began tearing up the old, groaning floorboards.

As he ripped through the layers, an old, forgotten mineshaft entrance was revealed beneath the floor. "Emma! Ben!" he shouted into the dark abyss, hoping for a response, but only silence greeted him.

"We need to get down there," John called out urgently, his voice thick with fear.

But before he could turn to search for a rope, a sudden push from behind sent both him and Mary sprawling forward into the newly uncovered opening. John whipped around, his eyes meeting those of Barbara, the cashier from J.R. Thomas General Store.

As John and Mary crashed onto the hard floor of the cave, their heads spinning from the impact, Barbara's voice floated down from the opening above, chilling and remorseless. "I'm sorry, but this is necessary. Father needs us, and we can't let him down. My daughter is already helping, along with Tony's girl. They know the sacrifices required to appease him. He demands a family, a commitment from all of us. It's the only way to keep him content. I'm truly sorry, but there's no other choice." Her words hung heavy in the damp air, revealing a twisted allegiance to the sinister legacy that haunted the woods around them.

"Barbara, please! Don't do this!" John's plea was desperate, a father's anguish filling the cavern.

Mary joined in; her voice raw with emotion. "Please, you don't have to do this! Let us go!"

But their cries for help were drowned out by the chilling sound of Barbara nailing the floorboards back down over the opening. Each thud of the hammer was a stark finality, sealing their fate as they lay in the dark, the reality of their situation closing in around them like the earthen walls of the cave.

Below, Emma finally caught up to Ben, grabbing his arm and pulling him to a stop. "Ben, we have to go back! That light—it's a trick by Harold to lure us deeper."

Breathing heavily, Ben's eyes filled with tears, the adrenaline fading as he realized the peril they had unknowingly sprinted deeper into. "I... I thought we could escape," he stammered, his voice breaking.

Emma hugged her brother tightly, her mind racing for any solution. "We'll find another way, Ben. We have to be smart, we have to be calm. Remember what Mom said? We can't let it win."

Back in the trapped space beneath the sealed floorboards, John and Mary clung to each other, the dim light of a single flashlight casting long shadows. Despite the dire circumstances, a resolve hardened within them—a determination to protect their children, to survive the machinations of Father, and to fight against the darkness that sought to consume them.

INTO THE ABYSS

In the oppressive darkness of the cave, John and Mary stumbled forward, the rough walls scraping against their hands as they blindly searched for their children. The air was thick with dampness, the silence broken only by their labored breaths and the distant drip of water echoing through the cavernous tunnels. With each step, the weight of the earth above seemed to press closer, a constant reminder of their entrapment.

As they ventured deeper into Harold's lair, strange, dissonant whispers began to fill the air, a cacophony of voices that seemed to come from nowhere and everywhere at once. The words were indistinguishable at first, but soon they morphed into the unmistakable sounds of Emma and Ben's voices calling out for help.

"Mom! Dad! Over here!" the voices cried, seemingly just around the next bend. Heart pounding, John raced towards the sounds, Mary close behind. But as they reached the spot where they believed their children to be, there was nothing—only the cold, mocking echo of dripping water.

"This way!" another shout, this time from a different direction. They turned and ran, desperation fueling their steps. Again, nothing but the empty darkness greeted them. The realization dawned slowly, a chilling understanding: Father was playing with them, using their deepest fears and desires against them.

"It's using our children's voices," Mary gasped, her voice trembling as she clung to John's arm. "It's... It's trying to break us."

John's eyes were wild with fear and determination. "We can't let it. We have to keep moving. We have to find them."

But it was relentless. The voices continued each call leading them further into a labyrinth of twisted passages and dead ends. With each step, the entity seemed to seep deeper into their minds, warping their perception of reality. Shadows flickered at the edges of their vision, shapes, and figures darting just out of sight, always elusive, always just beyond reach.

As the hours dragged on, the boundary between reality and illusion began to blur. Mary swore she could see Emma standing in a distant cavern, her face pale and eyes hollow. She ran towards her, only to find the vision dissolve into mist at her touch. John heard Ben's laughter, a sound so dear and familiar, echoing through a narrow passage. He followed the sound, only to find himself facing a blank, dead-end wall.

Their minds frayed under the constant assault, its whispers turning into screams, its invisible tendrils wrapping tighter around their sanity. It was like a parasitic entity, feeding off their despair, controlling their every move with the precision of a puppeteer.

"I can't do this anymore," Mary cried, collapsing against a damp wall. Her voice was hollow, defeated. "It's everywhere, babe. It's in my head. It won't stop."

John knelt beside her, his face drawn and pale under the beam of their dying flashlight. "We can't give up, sweetheart. This is what it wants. We have to fight it. For Emma and Ben."

But even as he spoke, doubt gnawed at him. How could they fight something that invaded their thoughts, that used their love against them? Father seemed to know their every weakness, every crack in their armor.

In the darkness, its presence grew stronger, its whispers turning into a chorus of torment. Mary and John huddled together, their flashlight flickering one final time before succumbing to the shadows. As the light died, so too did the last vestige of their hope, leaving them alone with the consuming entity that had ensnared them, its dark embrace tightening around their doomed souls.

John and Mary felt the final thread of their resolve fray and snap. Harold's whispers, once external invasions, now felt like their own thoughts, twisting and darkening with each passing moment. They clung to each other, not out of comfort, but out of a shared descent into madness, their minds no longer their own.

Sensing its victory, Harold tightened its grip. The once sporadic whispers became a constant stream of voices, echoing inside their heads. It was no longer just mimicking their children's voices but had begun to speak with their own, blurring the lines between self and other, reality and illusion.

Ben's eyes widened as he heard Harold's voice echo through the cave, chilling and authoritative. "Welcome to the family," Harold intoned. "You can all call me Father now."

Without hesitation, Ben, Emma, John, and Mary, their voices hollow, repeated in unison, "Father."

"Whatever you need from us, we are here for you, Father," they chorused, their words resonating through the cave.

Led through the winding, dark corridors, they clutched each other's hands in a tight, desperate bond. The reunion was devoid of joy or relief. Their eyes, once bright with life, now only mirrored the dim, eerie glow around them. Words were unnecessary; they understood they were all part of Harold now, bound together in endless night.

As they ventured deeper into the cave, guided only by the sinister voice of Father echoing through the dark corridors, his intentions became chillingly clear. "This town wronged me, treated me as a monster, and for that, they will feel my wrath for eternity. You, my new family, will help me exact my vengeance."

Mechanically, the family nodded, their expressions numb. Tears mixed with the grime on their faces—signs of distress that their dulled senses barely registered against the overwhelming oppression of the cave.

Father's voice led them into a large cavern that reeked of decay and dampness. "This will be your new home," his voice boomed from the shadows as if he were presenting them with a grand prize rather than their grim reality. The walls of the cavern were slick with moisture, and the faint dripping of water echoed ominously in the background.

John, Mary, Ben, and Emma stared blankly at their new living quarters, unable to protest. They were too broken, too far gone in their mental captivity to react significantly. The reality of their dire circumstances barely penetrated their consciousness.

As they tried to absorb their surroundings, the voices of the two girls materialized from a shadowy corner of the cave. "We're so happy to have more family," one chimed in, her tone disturbingly cheerful amidst the gloom.

"Come, let's show you around," the other added, taking Emma's hand with a grip that was both comforting and chillingly possessive.

Father's voice continued to resonate throughout the stone chamber, "You will learn to embrace this place, as I have. We are beyond the reach of time here. We are eternal, just like the torment I will inflict upon this town."

The family listened, tears streaming down their faces. Their bodies reacted with primal sobs to the horror of their situation, but their minds remained shackled by Father's influence, trapped in a perpetual state of obedience and despair.

In this vile sanctuary, dictated by Father's relentless commands, they were transformed from victims to unwilling instruments of his malevolent will, caught in an endless cycle of suffering and subservience.

To sustain itself and to continue feeding off their pain and suffering, Father devised a new role for them. Each night, as the world above slumbered under the moon's watchful eye, it sent them out into the woods. They moved silently, ghostlike figures drifting between the trees, their presence felt more like a chill down one's spine than seen with the naked eye.

In the eerie luminescence of the moonlight, John, Mary, Emma, Ben, and the girls converged on their target with grotesque gaiety. The night air, crisp and expectant, carried their low, discordant hums and bursts of laughter as they moved like shadows toward the unsuspecting home.

With a precise heave, John shattered the living room window, the loud crash cutting through the night's silence like a scream. Glass cascaded onto the floor inside, sparkling under the moon's cold gaze. They clambered through the broken window one by one; one of the girls, her grin wide and deranged, caught her arm on a jagged piece of glass. Blood welled up, bright and startling against her pale skin, but her smile only twisted wider. Unperturbed, she dipped her fingers into the crimson flow and began to streak the walls with her blood, painting ghastly symbols and patterns with a passion that matched the madness in her eyes.

Inside, their antics turned even more chaotic. They danced through the rooms, their movements sharp and erratic, singing twisted versions of nursery rhymes that warped the air around them. Their laughter echoed, a haunting soundtrack to the horror they were creating. Ben and Emma joined in, their innocence shadowed by the influence that pulled their strings, making them participants in the terrifying display.

In the master bedroom, Barbara and her husband lay huddled under the sheets, their faces etched with terror. The Harper family encircled the bed, caught up in a macabre dance led by the sinister influence of Father. Their voices formed a chilling melody that reverberated throughout the room, a cruel serenade for the trapped couple.

As they circled, one of the girls, her arm still bleeding, approached the bed with methodical steps. She reached out, her bloodied hand trailing ghastly red marks along the walls, symbols that dripped and streaked like the tears of the house itself. The marks seemed a perverse celebration of their captivity, a reminder from Father of his control and the broken promises he had made to Barbara about her daughter.

The scene was a twisted tableau, Father using the room to torment Barbara further, a stark reminder that her hopes of ever seeing her daughter again were as fleeting as the shadows dancing on the walls. His voice echoed through the chamber, a constant presence that mocked their despair, "This is where we build our family, Barbara. An eternal reminder of your loss and my victory."

"Remember us," they sang, their voices melding into a single eerie refrain that seemed to seep into the very foundations of the home.

As they left, retreating through the broken window, they placed the blood-stained doll on the porch which looked eerily close to the one that Tony described. The same one his daughter went missing with. Clothed in Ben's old shirt, soaked now with blood, it sat watching the dark street, a sentinel to their madness. Their laughter and songs faded back into the woods, carrying with them the nightmarish reality of their visit.

In the woods, the night closed around them like a curtain, the darkness of their actions blending seamlessly with the shadows of the trees. Father's presence palpated with satisfaction, its dark energy nourished by their depravity, binding them ever tighter to its will. They were no longer just a family lost to darkness; they were its emissaries, dancing on the edge of sanity, forever changed by Father's call.

As months turned into years, the story of the family consumed by the darkness in the holler was just another chapter in the local legend. New parents whispered to their children the tale of the lost family, cautioning them never to wander too close to the woods at night, lest they catch the eyes of the Father's sentinels.

Father, ever watchful and endlessly hungry, continued to feed on the family, sustaining them in a state of ghostly existence. They were neither alive in the traditional sense nor truly dead; they were something in between, something other—ethereal beings that haunted the border between the world of the living and the realm of shadows.

As the seasons changed and the years blurred into the timeless night, the family's true selves faded, leaving behind only the shells that Father needed them to be—eternal prisoners, forever part of the legend that kept the small-town whispering and watching the woods with wary eyes. Father had not just consumed their bodies; it had stolen their stories, their futures, turning them into mere characters in a tale of warning and woe, a cautionary story spun from the darkest threads of human fear and supernatural dread.

Review & Newsletter

T hank you for reading Within These Haunted Walls. If you enjoyed this book, please visit the site where you purchased it and write a brief review. Your feedback is important to me and I would love to hear your thoughts.

For new content and free short stories click the link below to join my newsletter. Be the first to know about exciting new book news and subscriber-only content.

https://dl.bookfunnel.com/5u57nso4xv

Printed in Great Britain
by Amazon